Death Takes Time

by the same author

RODERIC JEFFRIES

Death Takes Time

St. Martin's Press
New York

Library of Congress Cataloging-in-Publication Data

Jeffries, Roderic
Death takes time : an Inspector Alvarez mystery / Roderic Jeffries.
p.   cm.
ISBN 0-312-11260-2
1. Alvarez, Enrique (Fictitious character)—Fiction.   2. Police—
Spain—Fiction.   I. Title.
PR6060.E43D447   1994
823'.914—dc20   94-32250   CIP

First published in Great Britain by The Crime Club,
an imprint of HarperCollins Publishers

First U.S. Edition: December 1994
10 9 8 7 6 5 4 3 2 1

CHAPTER 1

Rivalry between the two villages, as different in appearance
as in character, was traditional and often sharp. Six kilometres apart, La Malon Haute, by several centuries the
older, was set on a sugar-loaf hill because when men had
founded it, safety had been by far the most important con-
sideration: from the hill, an approaching enemy would be
visible in any direction when still a long way away. However, once individual safety had become much less important, those who could afford to do so had moved and
founded La Malon Basse because on the plain a house was
no longer forced to be on many levels and cheek-by-jowl
with its neighbours; there, a man could prove his worth by
building wide.

The inhabitants of La Malon Basse sneeringly referred
to those from the older village as their poor country cousins.
The riposte was simple. Cousins perhaps, but from La
Haute. (A rather laboured play on the slang 'haute', the
smart set.)

Jospin, from the local Gendarmerie Brigade, swore as he
had to brake suddenly, having misjudged the corner,
despite his belief that he was a second Prost. What a hell
of a maze, he told himself as he changed down to first—
narrow, twisting roads, a cobbled surface that kept the sus-
pension thumping, and corners so sharp that a horse would
tie itself into a granny knot. He accelerated, changed up to
second, reached the last house and came to a stop. The
crest of the hill was now only a hundred metres or so above
him.

He climbed out and stared at the square house, built in
the dour local stone, which had umpteen roof levels because

of the degree of slope on which it was built. He'd heard that the village had become popular with artists and foreigners and that one of the largest houses had recently changed hands for one million five hundred thousand francs. It was difficult to believe even a foreigner could be that stupid.

The door was opened by a woman with an unusually dark complexion, very dark brown eyes, and jet black, straight hair, who wore an apron. 'Madame Benflis?' he asked.

She nodded.

'Where is she?'

'Out there, beyond the patio.' She pointed.

'Has the doctor been called?'

'They told me to telephone him, so I did. He said he'd be here immediately.'

She spoke French fluently, but with a noticeable accent; parents of mixed race, he decided. 'Will you take me through?'

He followed her across the hall, up two steps, and into a room that was on two levels. It was lightly furnished, suggesting impermanent occupation—bamboo table and chairs, a long, low pine sideboard, two woven wall hangings, a patterned carpet, and three framed, brightly coloured prints whose subjects were anybody's guess. Outside was a shallow patio, around the edge of which ran wrought-iron railings, and beyond that was a drop of some six metres. On the rocks below, a woman lay, face downwards, her head and shoulders in the shade of a cistus bush, the rest of her body in the sharp sunshine. A ragged pattern of blood ran from her head to the cistus. He turned. 'Exactly what happened when you arrived?'

She spoke haltingly and at one point seemed to be about to break down, but managed to regain her self-control. She worked five mornings a week for Mademoiselle Orr. This morning, she'd been a few minutes late because her friend's car had been very difficult to start—her friend, who drove her each morning from La Malon Basse, worked for Monsieur and Madame Fauroux. They were from Paris and behaved like it. Her friend said that they spent money like water and . . .

'You arrived here a little late. Was the house open?' he asked, cutting short what threatened to be a rambling description of the wealthy, arrogant lifestyle of the Parisians.

She'd rung the bell. There'd been no answer so, since she had a key, she'd let herself in. (She only did this when the mademoiselle was out.) First, she'd gone through to the kitchen to put on her apron and change her shoes. Then she'd begun to clean the house and because she'd not swept the patio for a couple of days—in fact, not since the southerly wind which had covered everything in a layer of Saharan sand—she'd decided to do that first.

To begin with, nothing had seemed to be wrong. But then, when halfway along the outer half of the patio, she'd paused for a moment's rest—in certain positions, her back became painful—and she'd looked below. Her distant sight wasn't all that good—but she could still read without glasses—and at first she'd thought it was a bundle of old clothes. Perplexed by the question of what they were doing there, she'd moved along the patio until directly above them and that was when she'd realized that what she was looking at was a body . . .

'Have you been down to make certain it's Mademoiselle Orr and that she's dead?'

She confessed that when it came to injuries, she was a total coward; nevertheless, she'd forced herself to go down to find out if there was anything she could do . . . There was no chance that anyone with such injuries could still be alive . . .

He thanked her, said he'd go down to look at the body.
She showed him where the concrete steps were—it was
difficult to know why anyone had built them down to the
rock ledge—and he descended these. The woman lay
almost on the edge of the ledge, her feet closer to the house.
The injuries to her head made him wince and he was not
surprised that Madame Benflis had been so positive there
could be no life left in the body. He straightened, turned,
and stared up at the patio. If the mademoiselle had been
standing up against the railings and for some reason had
overbalanced, she would have landed about where she now
lay.

There were voices, and then the rotund figure of Dr Parsec came into sight. He said something to Madame Benflis,
then climbed down the steps. 'I know you, don't I?' he
said, as he reached the ledge. 'It's Jospin?'

'That's right, Doctor.'

'Never forget a face,' he said with satisfaction. He studied
the body. 'How much do you know?'

'Just what the maid's told me since I've been here. All
she can say is that she arrived a little late, started work
sweeping the patio, saw the body and came down to check
there was no chance of life, then phoned for help.'

The doctor put down his bag and, after confirming death,
examined the body, discovering the extent of possible move-
ment—in turn, checking head, arms, and legs.

'What can you say about time of death?' Jospin asked.

'No more than usual. In this warmth, rigor can start
more quickly than usual, which probably means she died
between eight and twelve hours ago. But even that range
can still be wrong.'

'What about the injuries—are they consistent with fall-
ing from the patio?'

'As far as I can tell from a superficial examination, perfectly consistent.'

'There's nothing to suggest it wasn't an accident, then?'

'That's right. But to be certain, you'll have to wait on the PM . . . Well, there's nothing more that I can do here except give you a certificate of death, so let's go up top and I'll make that out.' He picked up his case and led the way across to, and then up, the concrete steps.

On the patio, in a part which had been swept, were two plastic chairs and a glass-topped, bamboo table. Parsec moved one of the chairs to bring it into the shade, sat, opened his case and brought out a form which he quickly filled in and signed with an illegible flourish. He handed the form across.

'Thanks, Doctor . . . Tell me something, will you? How easy would you say it would be to overbalance and fall from up here?'

He turned in the chair and studied the wrought-iron railings. 'It's all going to depend on height, isn't it?'

'The railings are quite high. How tall would you say she was?'

The doctor shrugged his shoulders. 'As she is right now, it's difficult to be sure. But one could suggest, fifteen centimetres shorter than you.'

Jospin stood against the railings. 'I'd have to lean out quite a way before I overbalanced, so she'd have to lean further. What could have made her do that?'

'That, surely, is a question for you, not me?'

'I'm wondering if she was too tight to know what she was doing?'

'Only the PM will give you a definitive answer . . . Why d'you think that she might have been that drunk?'

'Nothing, really, except that anyone who's sober is surely going to take great care not to lean out in the face of that kind of a drop?'

'So you're calling in the Sûreté?'

'I can't say I've decided yet.'

'You'll very soon have to.' Parsec stood. 'It's going to be hot today.' He looked at his watch, muttered something and left in a rush.

Jospin stood at the railings and stared at the body. If this were an accident, he'd receive no thanks for calling in the Sûreté; but if there was good reason for suspecting murder and he didn't, especially remembering that the death of a foreigner always had to be treated with extra care because it could cause unusual complications . . .

He found Madame Benflis in the kitchen. 'Tell me something about Mademoiselle Orr—was she a heavy drinker?'

'Not as far as I know. Why d'you ask?'

'It's difficult to think why she should have overbalanced and fallen unless she was too befuddled to realize what was happening.'

'All I can say is, I've never seen her so much as even a bit tiddly.'

'Have you tidied up anywhere inside the house?'

'Like I said, I went straight out to the patio and that's when I saw her.'

'You won't have cleared away any glasses or bottles?'

'That's right.'

'So I'd like to find out what's around.'

She looked at him for several seconds with a worried expression, then led the way out of the kitchen. The small dining-room was beyond the sitting-room, and on the round table were two empty bottles of wine, in addition to dirty plates, cutlery, and one glass.

'Even if the first bottle was far from full, she must have drunk quite a lot,' he said.

She shook her head.

'Maybe you just didn't know about her drinking because she made certain you didn't?' ·

'I suppose . . . Only one can usually tell.'

He wasn't nearly as certain about that as she seemed to

be. 'It's my guess that she drank too much wine, wandered out on to the patio and hadn't sufficient wits left to realize she was in danger of overbalancing.'

'I don't think . . . She wouldn't have been like that.'

'Why d'you say that?'

She shook her head again.

It would have been easy to dismiss doubts so inexact, but Jospin was a careful man. 'You must have a reason?'

'Well . . . it's like this, she was so scared of heights that normally she never went near the railings. Made me wonder why she rented the place. I mean, if she'd wanted somewhere on the flat, she could have found somewhere in La Basse.'

He wondered why she hadn't mentioned the dead woman's altophobia before?

CHAPTER 2

Poperon, an officer in the Police Judiciaire, was intelligent, sharp, hard-working, and possessed of very considerable ambition; and as if that were not enough to engender a sense of dislike amongst his companions, he had been born and brought up in Nice.

Madame Benflis opened the front door of Maison du Ciel (a ridiculous name, he thought). Automatically, he sized her up and placed her as either Algerian or of Algerian descent. 'Good morning. Sûreté.' He seldom wasted many words on an introduction. 'I'd like a word, if you don't mind.' His tone made it clear that he was not asking her if she did.

She led the way through the small hall into the sitting-room, with its view to the south of the wooded countryside.

'It's a very sad business,' he said formally, as he sat down.

She nodded.

'So I'm sure you'll understand that we have to find out how and why it happened.'

His abrupt manner worried her. 'I swear I don't know anything.'

'No call to get fussed, there's no suggestion you do.' That was not exactly true. Much to Poperon's surprise, the local gendarme, before reporting to the Sûreté, had had sufficient initiative to check that Madame Benflis had been at home with her family throughout the night of the Englishwoman's death. 'What I want to hear from you is anything and everything you know about Mademoiselle Orr. I'm told you've been working for her for some time?'

'I started soon after she came to live here.'

'And when was that?'

'I suppose it was a couple of years ago.'

'What was she like to work for?'

'All right. I mean, she never wanted me to do more than was reasonable and always paid on time. If she was going to be away, she left the money.'

'Was she a pleasant person?'

'Pleasant enough, but there wasn't much we could say to each other because her French wasn't good and I don't speak any English.'

'But in so far as you could understand each other, she was friendly?'

'I . . . I suppose she was.'

'You don't sound very certain?'

'Well, it's just . . . Now she's dead, it don't seem right.'

'To criticize her? Unfortunately, I have to know the truth. In what way was she unfriendly?'

'It's really nothing definite . . .' She came to a stop,

searching for words that would explain what she was trying to say.

Unlike Jospin, he found it difficult to be patient. 'What exactly are you getting at?'

'I suppose . . . It's really the way she was. Never really saying anything about herself. I know her French was terrible, but . . . And if she smiled, which wasn't often, her eyes never did. I don't suppose that makes sense?'

'What you're saying is, she was very much a reserved, private person?'

'That's right.'

'Then she maybe didn't have many friends?'

'She didn't, no. Sometimes someone would drop in and have a chat, but that's about all. Apart from the Englishman, of course.'

'Who's the Englishman?'

'His name was Bob.'

'That's a christian name, isn't it? What was his surname?'

'I only ever heard it the once. It was something like . . .' She thought, her eyes unfocused. 'Like Arles, only it wasn't that.'

'Tell me about him.'

'I suppose he arrived about a month ago. It was funny how things were between him and her.'

'In what way?'

'Well, when he first arrived, he asked for Mademoiselle Orr—in terrible French—and since I reckoned he must be a friend, I asked him to come straight in. But she didn't know him.'

'How can you be certain of that?'

'From the way things went. Maybe I couldn't understand the words, but I could see how they looked at each other and hear the tones in which they spoke.'

'Did he stay for long?'

'Not after she started shouting at him. She got so excited I thought anything could happen, but it didn't. So when he left, I said to myself, that's the last I'll be seeing of you. Which shows just how wrong one can be!'

'So he did come back?'

'The next day. And every day after that. And from the way they soon started looking at each other, it wasn't a surprise when he moved in.'

'What exactly do you mean by "moved in"?'

'What d'you think I mean?' she asked sarcastically, then suddenly became uneasy when she remembered to whom she was speaking. 'He was sleeping with her.'

'You're certain?'

'The two single beds in her bedroom were put together and his stuff was all around the place.'

'Things had changed from their first meeting, then?'

'These days, things happen quickly, especially with foreigners.'

'Where is he now?'

'I wouldn't know.'

'When did you last see him?'

'A few days ago when he'd packed and was about to go off to somewhere.'

'You've no idea where?'

'No.'

'Did you expect him to return?'

'He didn't pack all his stuff and after she'd driven him to wherever he went and had returned, she told me he'd be back soon. At least, that's what I thought she was saying.'

'Some of his stuff is still in the house?'

'That's right.'

'Show me where it is.'

She led the way up steep stairs and into a south-facing bedroom. 'I haven't tidied anything because I was told not to.'

He nodded. 'I'll have a look round so you might as well go back downstairs.'

After she'd left, he began his search. Amongst Mademoiselle Orr's clothes, in the built-in cupboard which ran the length of one side wall, hung a sports jacket and a pair of grey flannel trousers, the pockets of both of which were empty. In the bottom of the bow-fronted chest-of-drawers were two shirts, two pairs of men's pants, and three pairs of socks. He went through to the bathroom. Alongside containers of powder, hair shampoo, bath salts, and scent, was a spray-can of aftershave. The second bedroom proved to be empty of everything but the bed, cupboard, chair, and wardrobe. As he looked in the mirror on the door of the cupboard to check his appearance, he reflected on the fact that he had not come across a single personal item—no letters, address book, or diary, not even a snapshot that might open a tiny window into her past. This was sufficiently unusual to suggest she might be a woman who had carefully cut herself off from that past.

He returned downstairs to find Madame Benflis was using a long-handled brush to sweep the already clean kitchen floor. 'Do you know where the mademoiselle's bag is?'

'Over there, on the working surface.' She pointed. 'The other policeman said nothing must be touched so I've left it there.'

He crossed and picked up the handbag. Good quality but lacking elegance, like the clothes upstairs in the cupboard: very English. He opened it and spread the contents on the table. A little over a thousand francs in notes and coin, a small wallet containing a local guarantee card, a chequebook from the same branch of the Banque du Midi Basses-Alpes, a lace-edged handkerchief, a small French/English phrase book, and a key ring. There were five keys on the ring, but only one, because of its sturdy, complicated pattern, caught his attention. 'Is there a safe in the house?'

'Can't say I've ever seen one.'

Convinced the key had to be for a safe, he searched the house for one that was set in a wall and normally hidden. He found it in the built-in cupboard in the main bedroom. The key unlocked it. Inside was a small crocodile-skin case which contained several pieces of jewellery, garish rather than chic, a passport, two unused and one partially used chequebook from the Banque de Mont-Blanc in Geneva, and statements from that bank denominated in francs. He skimmed through the statements and immediately picked out a pattern. At the beginning of each month, twenty-five thousand francs were paid in; at irregular intervals throughout the month, that much was withdrawn. Was the source of her income a pension? At her age, that seemed impossible. Investments which paid a regular sum each month? He shrugged his shoulders. At the moment, the source of the money was not of any account.

He returned everything except the passport to the safe, locked that, sat down on the edge of the bed. There would seem to be some sort of a mystery about the dead woman since normally no one cut herself so completely off from the past. Had she had good reason to do so? Yet when a stranger had turned up at the house and logically she might have been expected to have had as little as possible to do with him, there had been initial argument but then she had received him into her bed . . .

He stood, put the passport into his coat pocket. Perhaps that would provide a lead into her past and her past would provide the answer to the present question: had she fallen or had she been pushed?

The house adjoining Maison du Ciel—though well below it because of the steepness of the land—had not been reformed and to enter it was to realize that while the past might be picturesque, it was often uncomfortable. Madame Mallet, with her ill-adjusted wig, wrinkled face, and arthritic limbs, looked almost as old as the house, but if her body was failing, her mind was not. 'I asked her one day, was she really paying five thousand francs a month rent? I told her, that was plain daft. Old Gaston would have taken three thousand if she'd argued.'

'Was she a friendly kind of a person?' Poperon asked.

'If I was sitting outside, she'd stop for a chat. Couldn't speak properly, of course. Sometimes I'd not understand a word she said.'

'When did you last see her?'

She considered the question, sucking at one of her three remaining front teeth as she did so. 'She went by yesterday afternoon.'

'Was she on her own?'

'That's right.'

'Did she stop and have a chat?'

'Only for a second. In a hurry, she was; said she had to drive to Auchoise.'

'Where was her car?'

'There's no garage at her place, so she rented one from Jean; that's Jean with the harelip. Paid him too much, same as old Gaston.'

'D'you think she was in a hurry because she was worried about something?'

'Might of been. Almost rude, she was, when I tried to tell her about Denise.'

'Who's Denise?'

'My niece.'

'In what way was Mademoiselle Orr rude?'

'She's been married for seven years with a couple of kids and that good-for-nothing husband leaves her for a strumpet. What d'you say about that?'

'Very sad. When you said "rude", what did . . .'

'I told her before she married Jacques. Your man needs watching. But she wouldn't listen. None of 'em listen these days, do they?'

'Very seldom,' he answered, trying to keep his impatience in check. 'Have you any idea why Mademoiselle Orr was in a rush?'

'No.'

'Or why she was driving to Auchoise?'

'How could I, when she didn't stop to talk?'

'Could she have been scared?'

'Scared of what?'

'I don't know.'

'Then why ask?'

'Let's talk about the man who was staying with the mademoiselle,' he said, both annoyed and amused by her. 'Have you spoken to him?'

'He'll stop and chat, only I mostly don't understand him because his French is even worse than hers.'

'Have you any idea what his surname is?'

She shook her head.

'What sort of a man would you say he is?'

'Bit ordinary, from the look of him—but he'd never leave his wife for a strumpet. After seven years, to leave Denise with two kids to bring up . . .'

He hastily interrupted. 'When you and she had a talk, did she ever speak about him?'

'Not really. I mean, if he wasn't with her I'd maybe ask how he was and she'd say, but that's all. Like when I didn't see him for several days and all she told me was that he'd gone away for a bit.'

'Then she didn't tell you where he'd gone to?'

'No.'

'Has she had any visitors recently?'

'All I've seen is the man who called at lunch-time.'

'When was this?'

'Yesterday.'

He tried to hide his increased interest. 'Someone visited her yesterday, at lunch-time?'

'Ain't that what I've just said?'

'Tell me about him.'

She'd been sitting outside when the car had driven past and come to a stop outside the mademoiselle's house. The driver had climbed out, knocked on the door, she had opened it and he'd gone inside.

'Can you describe him?' he asked.

She told him that her eyesight was good; her occulist said it was extraordinarily good for a woman of her age. Most people needed distance glasses very much younger . . .

'You're very fortunate. Now, about this man. What do you remember about him?'

He'd been young (to her, anyone less than late middle-age was as young as a spring chicken, he thought); tall and good looking; brown hair styled conservatively; a strong nose and a firm mouth; casual clothes with the cut of money (pretty soon, she'd be claiming to have read the Pierre Cardin label, he thought); the kind of man whom, had she been younger . . .

'Would you recognize him again?' he asked.

'That I would.'

'How long was he in the house?'

She shrugged her shoulders.

'You've no idea at all?'

'After my meal, the car was gone; that's all I can say.'

'How long after he arrived would this be?'

'Maybe an hour. I don't eat much these days. Not like when my husband always wanted a big meal . . .'

'I don't suppose you can tell me anything about the car?'

'It was foreign registered and had an E on the back,' she said triumphantly.

'Spanish!' His voice expressed his brief surprise. 'Would you have noticed the registration number?' he asked, with far more hope than would have been possible only a short while before. Typically this was to prove ill-founded.

'Can't say I did.'

'Or what kind of a car it was?'

'A white Ford Escort.'

'You are certain it was an Escort?'

'I've known cars ever since I was married and my husband, God rest his soul, worked for a very rich man who raced Delages and Delahayes. He was a marvellous mechanic, was my husband. Everyone said so.' Her eyes became unfocused as her mind drifted into the past.

He decided there was nothing more to be learned, stood, said thanks and goodbye.

'You don't want to see it, then?'

'See what?'

'The present she gave me when she came back from her holiday that time.'

'I really don't think . . .' he began, stopping as she awkwardly lifted herself out of the chair.

Once on her feet, she moved more easily. She left the room, to return with a small olive bowl in her arthritically misshapen hand. Lightly burned into the side of the bowl was, *Recuerdo de Puerto Llueso.*

Was it, he wondered as he read the words, pure coincidence that Mademoiselle Orr had had a holiday in Spain and that a man in a Spanish registered car had called at her house in the early afternoon of the day she died, or were the two facts connected? That probably depended on whether her death had been an accident or murder. But this was the very question he was trying to answer.

CHAPTER 3

The telephone woke Alvarez and he wondered resentfully who could be so ill-mannered and ignorant as to interrupt a man's siesta? Then the discomfort of the position he was in alerted him to the fact that he was not at home, in bed, but was sprawled out in the chair in his office. He opened his eyes as he struggled into a sitting position and stared at the pile of paperwork on the desk which he had resolved to start to deal with just before sleep had overtaken him . . .

The ringing had continued and finally he lifted the receiver.

'I am speaking on behalf of the Superior Chief,' said the superior secretary, sounding, as always, as if she had a mouthful of plums.

'Good afternoon, Señorita . . .'

She interrupted him with the rude disdain she had learned from her employer. 'Señor Salas has received a request, through the appropriate channels, from the French police. They wish us to establish the identity of a Spanish registered car which was seen in the village of La Malon Haute on Monday afternoon.'

'Surely it would be quicker to speak directly to Traffic . . .'

'The car is a white Ford Escort. The driver is probably English and may well live in or around Puerto Llueso.'

He reached across the desk for a pencil and turned over one of the many forms in front of him to use as notepaper. 'What is the registration number?'

'That is not known.'

'Then what else is?'

'Nothing.'

'But . . . but how can it begin to be possible to identify a car from so little information?'

'That is for you to answer, not me.' She cut the connection, naturally without bothering to say goodbye.

If he could work miracles, he would be farming a fifty-hectare finca, not slaving his life away in the Cuerpo General de Policia. Identify one white Escort from all the thousands on the island, knowing only that it might—or might not—belong to an Englishman who might—or might not—live in or near the port? His indignation lessened as he realized the task was so plainly impossible that not even Salas at his most illogical could condemn him for failing to accomplish it. Still, it would be best to give the appearance of trying to do something. He dialled Traffic. 'Inspector Alvarez, from Llueso. Will you be kind enough to identify the owner of a white Ford Escort who's probably English and possibly lives in or near Puerto Llueso.'

After a while, the man at the other end of the line said impatiently: 'Go on, then.'

'That's it.'

'You've a great sense of humour! What the hell's the registration number?'

'That's not known.'

'And you think we're going to kill ourselves working through the records to list all the white Escorts in your area.'

'It's Superior Chief Salas who thinks you will.'

There was a long pause. 'You know what your Superior Chief is, don't you?'

'I thoroughly agree.'

After the call was over, Alvarez thankfully settled back in the chair. Traffic would produce a list to cover themselves, he would investigate some of the names on this to cover himself, Salas would report to France that everything possible had been done—unfortunately without result—to cover himself. A reasonable solution.

He looked at his watch. In little over an hour, he could leave and return home. What might Dolores be cooking for supper? A surprise? Anfós amb tomàtigues?

The mortuary was on the outskirts of Sarignan, it's true nature tastefully concealed under the appearance of a bungalow, in front of which was a lawn that was maintained to bowling green standards.

In the autopsy room, the pathologist stripped off gloves, gown and cap and dropped them into a bin with a lid worked by a foot pedal. He crossed to the larger of the sinks and washed his hands with the same controlled, precise movements with which he dissected a body. He dried his hands on a paper towel, carefully inspected his nails. 'Right, gentlemen.'

The other six present heaved silent sighs of relief; this man who made a god of routine was finally ready to report his findings.

'I am unable to come to any definite conclusion. The injuries to the head occasioned by the fall were so severe that it is quite impossible to judge whether she had suffered any other injury, such as a blow, prior to the fall.

'There was bruising over two areas of the body; on the back of the shoulders and across the stomach. The bruising on the shoulders was light and patterned. As you will have observed, I asked my assistant—who has a larger hand than mine—to spread out his fingers and place them on the back to see if the pattern they formed matched that of the bruising. To a large extent, it did. Even so, I am not prepared to state categorically that prior to her death, force was applied through someone's fingers on her back.

'The heavier bruising on her stomach runs horizontally. Measurements from her heels to the marks correspond with the height of the horizontal bar of the railings surrounding the patio. My opinion is that this bruising was caused when she came up against the rail with sufficient force to cause her to topple over.

'Samples have been taken and will be sent to the laboratory. Tests on these will determine whether at the time of death she was under the influence of drink or drugs, or both. That is all.'

Poperon, choosing his words carefully, said: 'Monsieur, do you believe it probable she was pushed to her death?'

'I do. But I stress again the fact that that is an opinion, not a judgement.' His tone suggested that nevertheless his opinion was more to be relied upon than another man's considered judgement.

A week after the post-mortem, Poperon received the reports within a couple of hours of each other.

The deceased's blood/alcohol level had been .2 per cent. Such a concentration in a female subject denoted a marked state of inebriation.

The English authorities reported that the passport in the name of Bridget Orr was one of twelve which had been stolen in transit between the UK and the British Embassy in Germany some three years previously. Knowing that the French police were trying to determine the deceased's background, inquiries had been carried out and birth certificates relevant to the details entered on the false passport had been checked. As the French police would know (an Anglophobe could read into this the insolently superior belief that the French police would not know) in such a case as this, true personal details were often given by the criminal in order that he or she should have no trouble in remembering them if challenged. Unfortunately, it had proved impossible to gain any lead to the true identity of 'Bridget Orr'.

Poperon sat back in the chair and fiddled with his upper lip. Madame Benflis said that Bridget Orr had normally drunk very little. Yet on the night of her death, two empty bottles of wine had been on the dining-room table and it was now confirmed she had been drinking heavily. So had she been inveigled into drinking far more than she normally would and then, too befuddled to be suspicious until too late, had she been drawn out on to the patio and pushed over the railings?

Who was she? A false passport inevitably suggested a criminal background. Was a motive for her murder to be found in such background?

Assume she had been murdered. Who was the murderer? Bob, who'd turned up at her house a stranger and whose presence had initially been unwelcome yet who had nevertheless soon become her lover? He had left her house a few days before her death. In order to try to prove an alibi for a murder he would commit when he returned unseen? If so, then the visit of the man in the Spanish registered Escort on the afternoon of her death was coincidental. Yet this was the kind of coincidence that any detective viewed with suspicion even while he reminded himself that coincidences were two a franc . . .

Because there was a great deal of other work in hand, and because there was no immediately promising lead, he was unlikely to have nearly as much time for this case as it needed . . . He was by nature an optimist. If the white Escort were traced, and from that the driver's identity established, at least some of the facts would become known; perhaps enough to solve the case. He visualized a Spanish detective working just as hard as he would have done in order to uphold the honour of his force, had such a request been received from Spain . . .

CHAPTER 4

Man should not live by work alone. Alvarez looked at his watch. An hour and a quarter before he could safely leave the office and return home for Saturday lunch, which was often rather special. Although a woman, and therefore both illogical and irrational, Dolores was a wonderful cook. A man could forgive a woman much if she knew how to cook lechona so that the crackling, redolent of the spicy sauce, immediately shattered between one's teeth and the meat was as tender as a virgin's breast.

He resumed his tidying up of the papers on the desk and almost immediately came across the letter from Traffic which contained an endless list of car registration numbers, addresses, and names that he had put on one side several days ago, daunted by the task of dealing with it. So now what? Forget it again? But Salas might demand to know how the inquiry into the white Escort was progressing and so something had to appear to be done. Yet if he were to check on even half the numbers listed, he'd have no moment of rest between now and the end of the summer . . . He suddenly remembered that when he'd opened the letter on its receipt and had dispiritedly studied the length of the list, he'd noticed that a number of the cars were owned by the two largest hire firms in the port. So if he talked to the owners of those, he could then truthfully claim to have checked up on a sizeable proportion of the cars listed . . . And if he went down to the port now, he'd be back home in time for a drink before Dolores dished the Lucullan meal she was undoubtedly now preparing . . .

In the season, only one thing was scarcer in the port than altruism and that was parking space and in the end he had to settle for a solid yellow line, hoping that the municipal police would recognize his car. He locked the doors, turned and stared across the beach at the harbour, filled with power and sail boats. How much wealth lay on the water? How many tens of millions of pesetas did a man have to possess before he could with equanimity buy a boat which he used for perhaps no more than two or three weeks in a year? Was it not absurd that so much wealth should be left idle when it could be invested in land and the production of food? Yet the Common Market was organized, or disorganized, to produce so much food that there were already mountains of everything and therefore the man who wasted his money in idleness was more welcome than the one who made it work. Sweet Mary, but the world had become so complicated that a simple man was totally bewildered . . . His gaze wandered from the boats to the beach. Many of the female sunbathers were not only topless, but such scraps of costume as they wore left the imagination unexercised. Yet not that many years before, a woman in a generous two-piece costume would be ordered to dress respectably or suffer arrest for immoral behaviour. It was a world in which there was no end to the complications . . .

He crossed the road and made his way past tourist shops to the largest of the port's car hire firms. Lopez, the owner, was in the office. Small, with a wizened, pock-marked face and a mouthful of gold-capped teeth, even his friendly expression suggested he would find it easy to swindle his grandmother.

'What the hell do you want?' He ostentatiously slammed shut the cash drawer and locked it.

'Some information,' Alvarez replied equably.

'I don't know anything about anything.'

'There's no call for panic. I'm not interested in how much you're taking the tax collector for.'

'I pay those bastards everything I owe them.'

'Is that according to your reckoning or theirs?'

'Information about what?' Lopez asked, shifting the conversation away from a potentially embarrassing subject.

'I'm trying to trace who was driving a Spanish registered white Escort twelve days ago in La Malon Haute, in France.'

'Are you crazy? Who's going to hire one of my cars to go driving in France?'

'Only an optimist with no mechanical knowledge ... Here's a list of numbers I'm interested in. And the date at issue is the third of this month.'

Lopez took the list, but did not immediately look at it. 'You really think someone could have taken one of my cars to France? They're not insured off the island.'

'And most of 'em aren't insured on the island, either.'

'That's libel.'

'The rumour's wrong? You don't charge the customer full insurance for the hiring, but forget to account for that to the insurance company if he returns it undamaged?'

'That would be criminal!' Lopez said, striving to impart an expression of law-abiding surprise at the possibility. He crossed to the filing cabinet, pulled open the top drawer and brought out a partially used book of hiring slips. 'Do you want the names of everyone who had one of the cars on the third?'

'And the address and the date the car was returned.'

He checked through the carbon copies, writing from time to time. Finally, he shut the book and handed Alvarez a sheet of paper.

'Thanks. I'll do you a favour some day.'

'I'd feel happier if you don't,' he replied ill-naturedly.

Alvarez returned to his car and drove along the front to the miniature roundabout and then turned right on to the Parelona road. Half way along, ignoring a one-way sign, he turned left. Several years previously, this area had been green fields, now it was a gridiron of roads, shops, ugly apartment blocks, and houses, many of which were unfinished because of the recession. The port had possessed a quiet charm which had been treasured by the more discerning holiday-makers, now it presented much the same anonymous suburban sprawl that many of the less favoured parts did. The destruction had been carried out in the name of improvement. Could not someone have had the wit to understand that the quiet, undeveloped charm had been the port's most valuable asset? As he parked in front of an office whose window was plastered with posters proclaiming that here was to be obtained the best bargain for cars, he acknowledged that he was naïve even to pose such a question. It had never been a lack of forethought, but a surfeit of interests. Development meant money, man hungered for money so that he could buy a boat which he then left idle for months, thus helping the country not to grow more food . . .

He entered the office. The man behind the desk said: 'Enrique! Not seen you in a couple of full moons. What have you been doing with yourself?'

'Overworking.'

After they'd discussed mutual friends and the state of the world as it affected the island, Alvarez explained the reason for his visit.

'No problem. I'll check out the names for you right now.'

Some ten minutes later, Alvarez left. He drove through the side streets to the Llueso road and as he passed the petrol station and the last of the blocks of apartments, his good spirits returned. Mammon might have destroyed the coastline, but not the interior. Here, the countryside had hardly changed. Even Llueso, half ringed by mountains, had grown but not altered in essentials; at heart it was still a Mallorquin village and if it suffered tourists during the day, they were mostly gone by the night and, equally important, a coffee and a brandy did not cost five hundred pesetas . . .

He parked outside his house, walked through the front room and into the dining-room which was also used by the family as their everyday sitting-room. Juan and Isabel were watching the television, Jaime was seated at the table on which were a glass and a bottle of brandy. Alvarez sniffed the air, but could reach no conclusion as to what was cooking. 'What's for lunch?'

Jaime shrugged his shoulders.

He could, of course, go through to the kitchen and ask Dolores, but there was never any certainty as to how he would be received. If she was in one of her moods, the question might provoke her anger. Better to wait in expectancy. He opened a door of the sideboard and brought out a tumbler. He sat, filled the tumbler with brandy, drank. 'I've had one hell of a day!'

'Who hasn't?' muttered Jaime.

'I had to rush down to the port and have a word with Gaspar. He says that Lorenzo's eldest is going to marry Eulalia.'

'Then he's an even bigger bloody fool than I thought.'

'She seems nice enough, though.'

'But what about in twenty years' time when she's maybe more like her mother?'

Dolores, who had appeared unheard in the doorway, said: 'If who becomes more like her mother?'

Jaime, carefully not looking at his wife whose handsome face was flushed from the heat of cooking, muttered: 'Eulalia.'

'Eulalia Llabres? If she becomes more like her mother, her Pascual will be a very lucky man.'

'That's kind of what I was saying.'

She half turned. 'Enrique, are you ready to eat, or would you like a little more time to drink?'

He was so surprised by the courteous question that it was several seconds before he answered. 'Would another five minutes upset the meal?'

'Of course not.' She returned into the kitchen.

Jaime, in a low voice that was tinged with worry, said: 'She's been acting odd all day. God knows what's got into her.'

'She's not feeling ill?'

'She's not said she is. You don't think she could be kind of changing and becoming more understanding?'

Alvarez did not answer. There was no foretelling either the path of a mountain wind or the course of a woman's mind.

She shouted from the kitchen that someone should lay the table and a few minutes later carried in an earthenware pot which she put down on a board. When she saw the table had not been laid, she quickly set out mats and cutlery, but did not berate the two men for their laziness. They looked at each other. She lifted off the lid of the pot and a rich, complicated aroma spread through the room. Arroz a la Mallorquina. A dish originally designed to make the best use of the meagre food available to a peasant's home, but in skilled hands one that would not insult a king's table. Alvarez drained his glass, refilled it with wine, and waited impatiently to be served. As a plate was handed to him, the phone rang.

Dolores, about to serve Jaime, looked up. 'Isn't anyone going to answer it?'

'It won't be for me,' Alvarez said, before he ate the first mouthful of savoury rice, pigeon, peppers, garlic, mussels, fish, and sobresada.

She looked at her son. 'Go and see who it is.'

'But I'm hungry . . .'

'Please.'

Juan, perplexed by the request when he would normally

have received a sharp command, got down from the table
and went through to the front room. When he returned, he
said: 'It's for you, Uncle.'

'Didn't you say I was eating? Anyway, who is it?'

'I don't know. He just said he must talk to you.'

Alvarez helped himself to wine and another spoonful of
arroz, went through to the front room and the telephone.

'This is Doctor Garcia speaking. Come immediately to
the home of Señor Robson.'

'Is there some sort of trouble?'

'Would I be telephoning you if there were not. The señor
is in a coma from which he may well not recover and the
symptoms suggest poisoning.'

Alvarez sighed. 'Whereabouts is the house?'

'In the Laraix valley, along the road over the torrente.
It's behind the oaks; Ca'n Quirc.'

'I'll be there as soon as I can make it.'

He returned to the dining-room and sat.

'Who was that?' Dolores asked.

He swallowed his mouthful. 'Doctor Garcia.'

'Are you ill?' Her concern was immediate. The slightest
threat to anyone in her family panicked her.

'Not me. He wants me to go to the home of a foreigner
who's been poisoned and is maybe dying.'

'Thank God that's all it is,' she said, greatly relieved.
'My horoscope said that if I had a friendly day, I'd have
a friendly month.'

CHAPTER 5

When half way along the valley, Alvarez turned off the
Laraix road on to a metalled track which crossed the torrente and then wound its way between fields. A kilometre

and a half on, he rounded an orange grove to come into sight of a circle of evergreen oak trees. Instinctively, he slowed right down and as he came abeam of the oaks, crossed himself. He was a modern man and therefore naturally held ancient superstitions in contempt. Nevertheless, only a fool deliberately picked up a scorpion with a bare hand. Anyone over seventy knew for fact (as he'd been told by his father) that the oaks had been planted by the devil and a man had only to stand in the centre of the circle and make a wish for this to come true. So unless he called upon God to protect him, he was drawn by his desires to enter and wish, oblivious to the fact that the price of satisfaction was his soul.

Four hundred metres past the oaks was an arrow signpost listing Ca'n Quirc. He turned on to a dirt track which, because of the increasing gradient, doubled back on itself twice before coming to wrought-iron gates. On his close approach, they opened automatically. Beyond was a belt of pine trees and then the track debouched on to a large, natural rock shelf. On this stood a modern house, typical in design so that it appeared to be a series of units with different roof levels rather than a homogeneous whole, surrounded by a garden, the construction of which must have called for an endless amount of good earth. In front of the house were a new Volvo shooting brake and a battered Seat 127. He parked by the Volvo, climbed out, and turned to stare at the valley. Below were fields that were heavy with crops because the land was rich in underground water. On the far side, the mountains had saw-toothed crests, providing a dramatic skyline. To live here was to live with eagles.

He walked across to the front door and rang the bell. Seconds later, the door was opened by a middle-aged woman whose face, possessing more determination than grace, bore the marks of endless hours spent in the sun in earlier days. He was about to introduce himself when she said: 'Enrique, isn't it terrible!'

He struggled to identify her as he stepped inside.

'To think that only yesterday he was laughing, but now he's lying there, not moving a muscle.' Her eyes were red.

He remembered. Luisa Galmes. 'He's still alive, though?'

'But for how much longer?' She gestured with her hands. 'The wings of death are very close.'

Emotionally, Mallorquin women were exaggerated pessimists. (A conclusion he'd never passed on to Dolores.) But since life forced them to be practical, their grief was quickly assuaged unless a close relative were involved. 'One will just have to keep hoping. Where's the doctor?'

'He was in the sitting-room . . .'

Her reply was interrupted, and rendered unnecessary, when a door to their left was thrown open and a slight figure appeared. 'So you've finally arrived? Good God, man, if I responded to an emergency as quickly as you, half the population of Llueso would be in their graves.'

'I'm sorry about the delay, Doctor, but just as I was leaving the house there was a spot of trouble that had to be sorted out then and there.'

Garcia made a sound which could have been expressing either acceptance or disbelief, turned on his heels and went back inside. Alvarez nodded at Luisa, went into the sitting-room. It was large and filled with light, despite the patio roof which kept the window in shade. Furnishings and furniture were of good, often luxurious quality and even the television, video, and hi-fi equipment were sculptured rather than shaped merely for practical requirements. At first glance, the only touch of tastelessness were the wooden figures of Don Quixote and Sancho Panza which stood on the marble mantelpiece and this merely because every memento shop on the island sold such figures, crudely conceived and carved . . . Yet those with eyes to see what was, rather than what they expected, could appreciate that these two figures, far from being crudely mass-produced, had been sculpted by a master woodcarver.

Garcia stood in front of the fireplace in which had been set a wood burning stove, hands clasped behind his back. Alone amongst the doctors of Llueso, he dressed formally, no matter what the temperature. 'Do you know Señor Robson?'

'I don't think so.'

'I've not met him before today. The maid telephoned me to say he seemed very ill and would I come immediately. Because of her manner, I have to admit that I assumed she was panicking needlessly, but when I arrived it was to find that the señor was indeed a very sick man. Naturally, I called an ambulance and he was driven away some time before you belatedly turned up.'

'As I said, Doctor, I tried to get away immediately . . .'

'He was in a deepening cyanotic coma, the pulse had slowed, his body was growing cold, he was in a period of Cheyne-Stokes breathing, and his pupils were so contracted that the description, pin-point, wasn't as absurd as is usually the case. These, of course, are the classic symptoms of heroin poisoning.

'I gave what treatment I could—washed out the stomach with a touch of anaesthetic to seal off the glottis—but I'll be surprised if he lives.'

'Then he's an addict who's overdosed himself?'

'Probably a totally incorrect diagnosis. He's in very good physical condition and shows none of the signs of deterioration or damage that accompanies addiction.'

'Perhaps it was his first fix and he didn't know what he was doing?'

'Perhaps.'

'Where was he when you saw him?'

'Where the maid found him, on his bed.'

'Is there a hypodermic syringe in the bedroom; any sign of what the heroin might have been in?'

'I saw neither, but since it was not my job to do so, I did not make a careful search. But it is my job to advise authority of events which may well be of a criminal nature. Which is why I called you in . . . I must be off. Due to the length of time I have been forced to wait here, I have a great deal of work to catch up on.' He strode past Alvarez and through the doorway. A moment later, the front door was banged shut.

Alvarez, not aware he was doing so, shook his head as he pursed his lips. Despite what the doctor had said, the most likely explanation of events was that Robson had accidentally overdosed. This house suggested he was a wealthy man. How could someone who had so much endanger it by becoming an addict or, alternatively, experimenting with the drug when he must have known the probable consequences? So often, wealth seemed to carry a self-destruct button.

He returned to the hall and called out. Luisa entered through one of the doorways. 'How is the señor?'

'Doctor Garcia says he's seriously ill and only time will tell how seriously.'

'How could a man so fit yesterday be so ill today? Why, when I arrived . . .'

He listened patiently, even when she repeated herself. Yesterday, the señor had been laughing, active, his normal self. He'd spent time practising his golf swing, he'd weeded one of the flowerbeds—ever since Florit had left, the weeds had flourished—he'd had a long swim; he'd changed the gas cylinder for her when the stove had gone out, although she'd assured him that she was more than capable of doing that . . .

'Did the doctor tell you what he thought the señor was suffering from?'

She shook her head. 'Of course not.'

The doctor, the priest, and the lawyer; the aristocrats of the old days when they'd been the only people who'd eaten meat regularly. For some, they still enjoyed a social superiority so great they could not be expected to be forthcoming with an ordinary villager. 'Probably it's heroin poisoning.'

'Mother of God!' She stared at Alvarez for a while, then said: 'That's impossible.'

'Why d'you say that?'

'How can anyone imagine the señor would touch such wicked stuff?'

'Sadly, any number of people do these days.'

'Only those who are weak, like Julian, who has made himself stupid. The señor is strong.'

'The doctor said he could be wrong . . . Tell me exactly what happened this morning when you arrived?'

'I only do the cooking on a Saturday and he'd phoned to say he wanted a late lunch because he was playing golf in the morning and not the afternoon on account of the other señor having to do something later on. So I didn't arrive here until near midday. I got everything ready and I'd still some time to do so I reckoned on a bit of dusting, even though it was a Saturday.'

'Up until now, you'd not heard anything to suggest he was in the house?'

'Of course I hadn't.'

'So where did you start work?'

'He never makes his bed, so I went straight up to the bedroom. And . . . and there he was.'

'A very nasty shock,' he said solicitously. 'When did he phone you to say he wanted that late lunch?'

'This morning.'

'Fairly early on, presumably?'

'It was maybe about nine,' she answered, vaguely enough to suggest that it could have been noticeably earlier or later.

'How did he sound?' The question perplexed her. With continued patience, he explained what he meant—had the señor seemed at all upset, had he spoken in an odd manner, perhaps slurring his words?

'He was the same as ever. Talking odd Spanish, but working for him like I have, I've learned to understand him most times.'

'He didn't say anything to suggest he might be feeling ill?'

'No.'

'Do you know who he'd been expecting to play golf with?'

'Not really, but it could have been the señor who comes here and they practise with funny balls full of holes which don't go very far, which they mustn't, with the cliff so close.'

'What's this other señor's name?'

She thought for a long time, her broad brow furrowed. 'Señor Tait,' she finally said.

'And they're good friends?'

'Like I said, he's often here, on his own or with his señora. I think it's him who said to try the new kind of pills which helped the señor so much when the pine trees were in flower and he was sneezing like he was going to explode.'

'If I ask you what kind of a man Señor Robson is, how are you going to answer?'

She was reluctant to judge, but his friendly assurances soon overcame that reluctance. The señor, unlike those many foreigners who thought that when they employed someone they thereby proved their superiority, had always treated her more as a friend than an employee. In the past, she'd worked for other foreigners and naturally had always asked them to her husband's Saint's Day—they had either ignored or forgotten the invitations, but he hadn't. He'd turned up with a whole crate of Codorníu Non Plus Ultra and had spoken to everyone, though his Spanish had been even worse then than it was now and it had sounded some-times as if he were talking Greek. Tía Magdalena still laughed about that evening when he'd said something rude without meaning to . . .

'He sounds a nice man so let's hope he pulls through. I'd like now to have a look around his bedroom, so will you show me where it is?'

She faced him, hands on hips. She could hardly have looked more dissimilar to Dolores—even a Frenchman would not have called her handsome—yet there was something about her which irresistibly reminded him of his cousin; perhaps it was the aggressive certainty that, being male, he should not be left to his own inane judgements. 'He would never touch heroin; never.'

As he followed her out of the room and up the wide stairs, he wondered how much credence to place in her judgement? Having worked for Robson for some time, she must know quite a lot about him, but did anyone—even a husband or wife—ever know another so well that he or she could guarantee what that other would do, or not do, in all circumstances and at all times? On the other hand, a man on drugs must have difficulty in hiding his addiction from someone who saw him six mornings a week and could therefore judge what were his normal ways and habits.

The bedroom was almost as large as the sitting-room. The bed was unmade and bore witness to what had occurred.

She said: 'I wanted to take everything off and put it in the washing-machine, but the doctor told me I mustn't.'

'He was quite right. When you first saw the señor, he was lying on this bed, as far as you could tell, unconscious?'

She nodded. 'Enrique, I need to go home. I phoned Felix and told him about the trouble, but like as not he's not got his own lunch.'

'Then go on back home. And if he wants to know why you've been so long, tell him we've been busy in the bedroom.'

She smiled, but only briefly. Like most Mallorquin women, she enjoyed a joke of earthy quality, but the events of the morning were still sufficiently close to make her feel that levity was misplaced.

After she'd gone, he searched the bedroom for the tools of an addict. He found no hypodermic syringe, no primitive 'outfit'—safety-pin, eyedropper, spoon, and cotton-wool— no container which might have held heroin. In the adjoining bathroom, notable for the pattern of the wall tiles, and the dressing-room, he again drew blank.

He widened his search, taking in the other four bedrooms and bathrooms, the dining-room, breakfast-room, sitting-room, library, kitchen, and utility room. He went outside and emptied the dustbin and checked the contents. He examined from bonnet to boot the Mercedes in the garage. He scoured the garden.

Back in the sitting-room, he settled on the settee, lit a cigarette. When a man took a fix, he usually did not— frequently could not—move again until the effects had worn off. So if the house had been thoroughly searched, which it had been, and nothing had been found, which it hadn't, one had to postulate Robson's giving himself a heavy fix, leaving the house and grounds to hide the evidence, and then returning inside and going upstairs to his bedroom. Which seemed absurd. Doctor Garcia had said there was no external evidence on Robson's body of addiction. Assuming he was not an addict, then a dose of heroin would hit very hard, very quickly; so hard and so quickly he probably couldn't have staggered anywhere . . . Confirming a freedom from addiction, Luisa said he had showed none of the sharp swings of mood that one would have expected had he been an addict. Yet if he were not one, how and why had he come to ingest a dose of heroin so great that it might well prove fatal?

CHAPTER 6

Yawning, Alvarez climbed out of bed and slowly dressed. He went down to the kitchen.

'You look terrible,' Dolores observed.

'I feel terrible.'

'Because you drink too much.'

Only a few hours before, she had been encouraging him to have another brandy before lunch. Could a chameleon change its colour more quickly than she changed her mood? 'I feel terrible because I got back here so late there wasn't time for a proper siesta and I've had no more than a five-minute nap.'

'For the last hour, you've been snoring loudly enough to wake up the whole street.'

When she was in this kind of a mood, one could not reason with her.

'And now I suppose you expect me to make you hot chocolate?'

'There's no need for you to bother. I'll do it,' he answered hastily.

'And have my pots ruined? Sit down and just be grateful that I'm a dutiful woman who never complains, no matter how heavy the burden.'

He sat at the kitchen table. There was a time when silence was not only golden, it was also essential. After a while, she set in front of him a slice of strawberry sponge cake as well as a mug of hot chocolate. He ate and drank and began to feel more alive. Even the thought of all the work which lay ahead failed to dampen his mood.

*

He phoned Garcia at seven-thirty. 'Doctor, it's Inspector Alvarez. Have you any news about Señor Robson's condition?'

'Despite everything that could be done, he died just over an hour ago.'

'That's tragic.'

'Yes,' replied Garcia impatiently, too familiar with death to accord it any respect.

'Have you anything more on the cause of death?'

'Although it will require a post-mortem and subsequent forensic tests to establish certainty, you may accept it that he died from a massive overdose of heroin.'

'Did the clinic say whether he showed signs of being an addict?'

'Quite the contrary. They say that the evidence to date suggests he was not.'

'Suppose it was the first time he'd ever taken heroin, how soon would it begin to act?'

'Almost immediately.'

'He wouldn't have been capable of going out of the house, walking around for a while, then returning indoors and going upstairs to his bedroom?'

'Are you seriously asking such a question? Wasn't it obvious from the state of the bed that he was unable even to reach the bathroom?'

'The trouble is, I've searched the house and the garden and there's not a sign of a hypodermic needle.'

'Heroin can also be sniffed, rubbed into the gums, or taken orally.'

'Yet however he took it, it must have been contained in something. But there's nothing, anywhere. Unless, of course, he slipped the container into one of his pockets as soon as he'd emptied it and it's still in his clothes. I haven't had a chance yet to examine what he was wearing when he was taken to hospital.'

'Because you were unduly delayed . . . He was wearing only boxer shorts.'

'Then probably he'd just got up and was beginning to dress.'

'After either showering or bathing.'

'Are you assuming that?'

'I'm making a reasoned judgement in the face of the evidence of a towel draped over the edge of the bath.'

'I didn't see one.'

'I cannot say I am surprised.'

Garcia was known more for his skill than his bedside manner. 'Would you imagine that a man who intended to give himself a fix would bother about showering or bathing first?'

'When a man uses drugs, there is small point in searching for logic. Is there anything else, Inspector. I am a very busy man.'

Alvarez thanked him, said goodbye, replaced the receiver. He wondered if there was a good reason for not phoning Salas at home, but couldn't think what that might be. He dialled.

'Yes?' said Señora Salas and even with that single word she managed to convey a sense of all the superiority of a Madrileño matron.

Some impish sense of humour prompted him to reply to her in Mallorquin.

'Kindly speak so that I can understand you.'

Impish humour was seldom appreciated. He repeated what he'd said in Castilian. She ordered him to wait.

'What the devil is it?' were Salas's opening words.

'Señor, this morning, not long after midday, an Englishman, Señor Robson, was discovered by his maid to be in a deep coma on his bed. Doctor Garcia examined him, treated him as far as that was possible, and sent him to a

clinic in Palma. Unfortunately, the señor died. It is the
doctor's opinion, echoed by the clinic—though confir-
mation can, of course, only come from the laboratory—
that the señor died from a massive overdose of heroin. Yet
despite the fact that this probably affected him virtually
immediately, I have searched the house and garden and
found no trace of heroin, the container in which it was, or
the means by which it was administered. Further, his physical condition suggests he was not an addict. There does,
therefore, seem to be a mystery about his death.'

'If there weren't, you could be relied upon to manufac-
ture one.'

'I think it possible that he may not have killed himself
with an accidental overdose, he may have been murdered.'

'By whom?'

'I can't answer that yet.'

'Why not?'

'Señor, it's only an hour or so since he died. In so
short a time, surely it is impossible to ascertain sufficient
facts to be certain what happened, let alone suspect anyone?'

'It is my experience that the word "impossible" comes
most readily to the lips of those for whom very little is
possible. Next time, take the trouble to ascertain the facts
before you make a report.' He cut the connection.

Obviously, the Superior Chief had spent his time off
duty on the golf course, slicing, hooking, and becoming
bunkered.

Dolores hurried into the front room. 'I have to go out to
buy a barra for supper. Tell Jaime where I've gone if he
comes back and wants to know where I am.'

He watched her step through the bead curtain across the
front door. Had Jaime been at home, she would have
scorned telling him where she was going because that would
be to grant him the right to be told; but because he was

not there, she willingly acknowledged such right. Women would never cease to perplex him. He went through to the dining-room and poured himself a glass of brandy.

He awoke and gratefully remembered that it was Sunday. He could enjoy a few more minutes in bed which would help him overcome that period of disorientation that invariably followed an awakening; but not too many because Jaime and he had promised to strip down and paint the kitchen shutters. Not that he could hear any sounds to suggest that Jaime was up ... He closed his eyes and drifted back into sleep.

From the road, the terrace houses looked bleak, despite the painted shutters and window-boxes filled with flowers; yet in the past ten years, almost all of them had been reformed inside and now provided a comfort which had been un-dreamed of in previous generations.

Alvarez stepped through the bead curtain into the small entrada, called out. Luisa's eleven-year-old son, his square, bluntly featured face unmistakably marking the relation-ship, entered. 'Is your mother at home?' Alvarez asked.

'No.'

'Do you know where she is?'

'Yeah.'

'Then where?'

'What's it to you?'

'Cuerpo General de Policia.' If he thought the sonorous title would impress, he was mistaken.

'You don't look like a detective. More like old Julian who sharpens knives.'

It was a pity that it was no longer the custom to clip the ears of a precocious young boy. 'Well I am one, so you can tell me where she is right now.'

'Up at the house of the foreigner who's just kicked the bucket.'

'Have you no more respect for the dead than to talk like that?'

'Are you asking me to respect you, then?'

Alvarez returned to his car and settled behind the wheel. He was not surprised that Luisa was up at Ca'n Quirc. Were that his son, he'd seize every opportunity to be away. In any case, she would have heard of the death of the señor—Llueso's bush telegraph was far more efficient than its official one—and therefore she would want to prepare the house so that his body could be laid in state, should it be brought back from Palma, for his friends to pay their last respects.

He drove out of the village on to the Palma/Puerto road and along to the roundabout, left that on the Laraix road. The sky was cloudless, the sun pleasantly warm—the real heat would come in July and August—the crops were good, the animals fecund, and there wasn't a tourist in sight. Eden must have been like this before Eve reached for the fruit of the tree of good and evil.

He had made up his mind that this time he would not give way to superstition. Yet as he approached the circle of oaks, he slowed the car and when abreast of them, he crossed himself, consoling his conscience with the thought that insurance was a sign of prudence, not belief.

He parked by the Seat 127, walked up to the front door and into the house. From upstairs came the sound of a vacuum cleaner. He cupped his hands about his mouth and called Luisa's name, but had to repeat it three times before the machine was switched off. She appeared at the head of the stairs.

'Can you come on down and have a word?'

She descended the stairs, her expression worried.

'There are just one or two more things I have to check

up on with you. Tell you what, how about doing that over a cup of coffee?'

Some of the worry left her heavy face and she led the way into the kitchen. She separated the two halves of a coffee machine, filled the lower with bottled water, put two spoonfuls of ground coffee into the perforated cup which fitted into this, screwed the halves together and set them on a lighted gas ring.

'First off,' he said, 'I need to know whether, after the doctor arrived, you went into the señor's bathroom and moved a towel?'

She fidgeted with the corner of the apron she wore, finally said: 'Shouldn't I have done? I mean, the doctor didn't say anything about not moving things in the bathroom and I wanted it to be clean for when he washed his hands.'

'There's no call to bother and all I want to know is exactly what happened?'

The doctor had examined the unconscious señor; she, knowing the señor always started the morning with a bath or shower, had gone into the bathroom to tidy up; the doctor had come in to ask her something—she couldn't now remember what—she had removed the towel that had been left, as it usually was, on the side of the bath, and had taken it down to hang up on the line which was not in the direct sunlight.

'Was it damp?'

'Of course it was, seeing he'd been using it.'

Robson had left his bed and had a shower or bath. He'd dried himself on the towel. He'd begun to dress and put on boxer shorts. And then the routine had suddenly been shattered. Why? How? 'When you tidied up the bathroom, did you move anything that could have contained powder—a pill box, a small plastic bag, anything like that?'

'There wasn't nothing.'

'And no hypodermic syringe?'

She folded her arms across her ample bosom. 'I told you. It's daft, thinking he'd have anything to do with that stuff.'

'Yet it's all but certain that he died from heroin poisoning.'

That confused her and she unfolded her arms, fiddled with the control of the gas burner to make certain it was fully turned on.

'You liked him, didn't you? So perhaps you're trying to hide the fact that he had a pretty nasty secret?'

'I'm telling you, there was nothing.'

'If that's so, it's more than possible he didn't die accidentally, he was murdered.'

'Sweet Mary!' This was more a brief prayer for his soul than an exclamation of surprise. If there hadn't been something unusual about the señor's death, Alvarez would not have returned to ask more questions.

'So I'm going to need to know more about him—what sort of a man he really was, who his friends were, all that sort of thing.'

She went over to a cupboard and brought out of it two cups and saucers which she set on the table; to another cupboard for a silver bowl of sugar; and to the large, double-door refrigerator for a carton of milk. The coffee machine hissed and she waited a short while, then turned off the gas. She filled the cups with coffee. 'If this was my house, I'd give you a coñac to go with the coffee.'

'Was the señor a teetotaller, then?'

'Him—a foreigner?'

'If you're worried about him not being here to offer it himself, I'm sure he's regretting that he can't be.'

His certainty seemed to convince her. She left the kitchen, to return with a bottle of Torres' Hors d'Age brandy which she handed to him before opening one of the cupboards and bringing out two balloon glasses.

As he poured each of them a generous drink, she drew

up a second chair and sat. She helped herself to three spoon-fuls of sugar, stirred the cup, her mind elsewhere and her gaze unfocused. 'Seems kind of strange, the house being so quiet. He used to play music all the time when he didn't have guests. So loud I had to turn it down if I was in the same room because it hurt.'

'Did he have many visitors?'

'Enough to keep me busy since I did the cooking. If it was lunch, I'd stay on to serve; if it was dinner, I'd leave things so all he had to do was put them in the oven. He said I was a better cook than his wife ever was.' This clearly was a compliment she treasured.

'Does his wife ever come here?'

'I've never seen her.'

'Did he have a girlfriend?'

'Never known a man who didn't, given half a chance. Only with him, they came and went so quickly sometimes I hardly knew their names. Brazen about it, too. Putas, the lot of 'em; except for the last one, of course.'

'She was different?'

'She couldn't be more so. Not the kind to go swimming without a costume and doesn't spend all her time acting like she can't get to bed quickly enough.'

'From the way you're talking, she's still around?'

'She was here on Friday.'

'Do you know her name?'

'Señorita Honor Seymour,' she answered, emphasizing the 'señorita'.

'Where's she from on the island?'

'The port, but I can't say more than that.'

'Is she here on holiday?'

'If she is, it's a long holiday. She's been seeing the señor for weeks. And if you ask me, I'd say he was really keen on her.'

'And she was fond of him?'

She seemed about to answer, then didn't. She saw him looking inquiringly at her and said: 'She liked him. Maybe it was more, only . . . A woman can tell.'

He finished the coffee. 'You mentioned Señor Tait. Did he and the señor get on well together?'

'They saw each other often enough. And the señora made the señor laugh.'

'Have you ever known the señor to have a row with someone?'

'He wasn't really that kind of a person. He didn't get angry even when one of his women didn't want to leave and tried to make a scene.'

'It sounds as if you can't criticize him?'

'Not really.'

He hadn't missed the slight hesitancy. 'But he wasn't perfect?'

'Well, maybe he didn't get angry, but he could be sharp.'

'With you?'

'Never with me.'

'With whom, then?'

'It doesn't seem right, talking like this and him still not in his coffin.'

'I'm afraid you're going to have to tell me all you know.'

After a while, she said: 'It was with Florit, the gardener.'

'What happened?'

'The señor sacked him for stealing, only . . .'

'Only what?'

'Only Florit didn't steal and there was no call to sack him. So he took a few bulbs. Where's the harm in that when there were hundreds of 'em? And Florit was so stupid about getting caught, you'd have expected the señor to laugh, not get so sharp.'

'How was Florit found out?'

'Soon after the señor bought the house and me and Florit came and worked for him, he said he wanted daffodils in the spring and sent off to somewhere in Holland for 'em because the ones he could buy here weren't good enough for him. He'd had loads and loads of soil brought in by lorry and Florit had made flowerbeds and so when the bulbs came and he'd sorted things out with customs—and did that take a time!—he told Florit to plant 'em all out. When they came up they were lovely—I'd never seen such big flowers. Florit told his wife how good they were and she kept on and on about how much she wanted some in the patio at the back of their house, so when the time was right, and the señor was away, he dug up some bulbs, and it wasn't very many, and planted 'em back home.'

'So how did the señor find that out?'

'The bulbs Florit had taken multiplied and so this spring he had a lot more flowers than before. So he picked half the blooms and took 'em to the flower shop by the square and they bought 'em. That afternoon, the señor was passing by and saw 'em and wondered who else was growing the same special daffodils as he was and he went in and asked. They're from the Peninsula, so they told him.'

One had to be a peasant, or of peasant extraction, to understand why the taking of the bulbs had not been theft and why Florit, after doing all he could to please his wife, should then diminish that pleasure for the sake of a few pesetas. When a man like the señor possessed so much that he did not know when he'd lost a very small part of what he'd had, then no harm was done if he lost that fraction for the sake of giving pleasure to others. Those extra blooms had been a bonus, but one which did nothing to feed a man's belly. Even a few pesetas would help to do that. 'Did Florit try to explain the way things were?'

'The señor wouldn't understand. I mean, Florit couldn't say he hadn't taken the bulbs and that's all the señor was interested in. You'd have thought he'd have smiled and shrugged his shoulders, or even maybe given Florit some more bulbs for his wife, but he sacked him, just like that. Didn't pay him for the whole week, but only for the days he'd been here, and then even deducted what he said the bulbs had cost.'

'How did Florit react?'

'How d'you expect? Said a lot of things he shouldn't have done. But he said 'em in Mallorquin, so the señor couldn't have understood.'

'Did he threaten to kill the señor?'

She stared at him with growing, confused concern, suddenly aware of a possible interpretation of what she'd been saying. 'Mother of God, you've got it all wrong! Florit was upset, that's all.'

'Of course.' But a peasant's honour could be his most treasured possession. 'Did the señor treat anyone else like he treated Florit?'

'Who else is there but me and I've worked for foreigners long enough to know they don't think straight.'

'What about the women? Did he get sharp with any of them?'

She shook her head. 'I never knew that, not even when they were screaming at him. In fact . . .' She stopped.

'Yes?'

She said nothing.

'It's just between you and me.'

'Well, there were one or two times when I thought that maybe . . . That maybe he was even enjoying their going on like they were.'

Gaining pleasure from their misery? 'And there's no one else you can think of who might have disliked him?'

'Not really. Only the Englishman who arrived all of a state and shouting, but that didn't go on for long.'

'Tell me about him.'

'It was during the Calms of January when it was a lovely day and warm . . .'

Robson had arranged to play golf with Tait and had told
her there was no need to cook him any lunch. He'd put his
golf clubs in the back of the car and had returned to the
house for something when the telephone rang. She'd been
polishing the stairs and so had heard his end of the conversation. She had, of course, understood very little of what
he'd said, but his tone had made her think there was some
sort of trouble. When that call was over, he'd rung Tait
and this time she'd gathered enough to know that he was
saying he couldn't play golf at the time arranged. An hour
later, a visitor had arrived—she'd never heard his name.
And the moment he'd stepped out of his car, he'd begun
shouting so wildly, she'd feared there'd be a fight . . .

'But the señor wasn't angry?'

'I can remember thinking he seemed more amused than
anything, as if he'd a private joke.'

'And then?'

'The señor told me to make coffee. And you know what?
By the time I took it into the sitting-room, the Englishman
had almost calmed down.'

'Maybe the señor used the same technique that he did
with the ladies.'

She wasn't certain whether or not that question was
meant seriously.

'What happened after they'd had coffee?'

'They drove off, the señor in his car, the Englishman in
his.'

'Have you any idea where they went?'

'I couldn't begin to say.'

'Have you seen the Englishman again?'

She shook her head.

'Can you describe him?'

She had a peasant's memory for detail. Late middle-age;
medium height, overweight; brown hair receding and
beginning to grey; light blue eyes that seldom looked

directly at one; a bulbous nose which added a touch of the clown; clothes that could have been cleaner and neater. His car, a Renault 5, had seen much better days.

He wondered whether there was any connection between this man's visit in January and the señor's death in May?

CHAPTER 7

Alvarez rang the banks and the solicitors in Llueso and asked them if Señor Robson had been a client. One bank and one solicitor said immediately that he had not; the other banks and solicitors said that they could not give an immediate answer due to the pressures of work. As he replaced the receiver after the last call, he thought how laughable it was that such people should complain of overwork when they hardly knew the meaning of the word.

He sat back in the chair. In a while, he must drive down to the port.

Lopez, seated behind the counter in the office of his car hire firm, his expression bitter, said: 'Haven't you anything better to do than keep interrupting an honest man trying to earn a living?'

'It's a long time since I've had the chance to do that,' Alvarez replied. 'I'm trying to find the address of an English señorita.'

'And you're so thick you think this is a bloody information service?'

'I'm so thick I thought you'd rather help than have this place closed down for violating a dozen health and security regulations.'

'You know something? This was a far better country back in the days when people like you were kept in your place.'

'And you were a labourer lucky to earn a peseta an hour?'

Lopez swore.

'Is a Señorita Seymour hiring a car from you?'

Muttering, but not so loudly as to be understood, Lopez began to search through the records. After a while, he cleared his throat noisily. 'So what if she is?'

'You can give me her address.'

'Ca Na Antonia.'

'Which is where?'

'The urbanización at the back.'

The urbanización lay in rock-littered ground at the foot of the mountains. Initially developed by a man with ideas but little capital, the plots had been small to attract the less-than-wealthy buyer. Small plots had meant that small bungalows had been built, usually by off-duty waiters who'd thought a plumb line was the point of a joke. Time had not been kind to the area. Foundations—where there were any—had shifted, roofs had moved, walls had cracked, wood had warped, and paintwork had blackened from mould.

Alvarez parked outside a bungalow whose minute front garden was overwhelmed by a palm tree in its centre. He left the car, walked up the very short path, knocked on the front door. The door was opened by a woman in her middle-twenties and it took all his self-control not to gawp at her as if he were an inexperienced teenager. When he dreamed of woman spiritual, he dreamed of her. Tall, understatedly shapely, she had the face of a practical angel with a sense of humour. Her black hair was casually shaped about her head—but no hairdresser could have improved on its style—her eyes were blue and touched with a hint of violet, like the evening sky at the end of July, her nose had an impudent tilt at the end, and her lips were made for laughing love . . .

'Do you want something?' she asked in heavily accented Spanish.

He pulled himself together. 'Señorita Seymour?'

'Yes.'

'My name is Inspector Alvarez of the Cuerpo General de Policia,' he said in English. 'May I have a word with you?'

'Yes, but why? Or is it about Hugh?'

'I'm afraid it does concern Señor Robson, Señorita.' He suffered guilt because his questions could only cause her further distress. He would have given much not to have to ask her anything.

'You'd better come on in.'

He followed her into a room that had been furnished in garishly bright colours in a vain attempt to hide the fact that every item had been chosen for its lack of value and ease of replacement. He sat on a chair whose cushion covers had worn through in places. She should have been living in a marble palace, not this tired, tatty bungalow . . .'Señorita, may I say how sorry I am that the señor should have died.'

'Thank you.' She stared into space. 'It's been so terribly sudden. I was with him the day before and he was the same as ever, laughing, fun to be with . . .' She turned her head away and was silent for a while. 'I'm sorry,' she said finally.

'Señorita, there is absolutely nothing to be sorry about.'

'One can't rule one's emotions. When someone told me he'd been taken desperately ill and had been rushed into one of the clinics in Palma, it was rather like being hit in the stomach. I tried to tell myself that this was one more absurd rumour and that when I phoned his place he'd laugh when I told him what I'd heard . . . Only there was no answer. So I rang round the clinics and a woman at the Tamis told me he'd just died . . . I've tried to find out when the funeral will be, but no one seems to know. Can you tell me?'

'I regret, but it is impossible to say yet.'

'But I thought . . . I thought that here, because of the climate, a funeral had to be very quick.'

'Unfortunately, there can be no funeral until the cause of death is certain.'

'You're saying that it isn't?'

'There will have to be a post-mortem.'

'But I don't understand. What's so mysterious about a heart attack?'

'Both the doctor who attended him at his home and the staff at the clinic are of the opinion that he died from a drug overdose.'

'He wasn't ill, so why should he have been taking any drugs?'

'Not medical drugs, Señorita.'

'Then what are you talking about?'

'Heroin.'

'My God! . . . Are you crazy?'

'You find it difficult to believe?'

'Hugh never touched that sort of drug in his life.'

He chose his words carefully. 'Is it not rather difficult to be so certain of that?'

'No, it isn't. It's never difficult when you know someone well.'

'Which you did?'

She swung round and stared at him, then hurried out of the room. There were times, he thought glumly, when his job became a despicable one.

When she returned a few minutes later, her eyes were red. She sat. 'I'll try not to be so stupid again.'

Only the English could call natural emotions 'stupid'; he admired their cold self-control, yet was certain that warm indulgence was to be preferred because it was kinder.

'You're suggesting Hugh was a drug addict, aren't you?' she said challengingly.

'That has to be one possibility.'

'An impossible one. What are the others?'

'That he was murdered.'

'Why should anyone want to murder him?'

'At the moment, I have no idea.'

'It's a ridiculous suggestion. Why couldn't his death have been accidental?'

'It surely is difficult accidentally to take sufficient heroin to kill oneself?'

'I told you, he's never touched the stuff.'

'Señorita, I must ask you this. How well did you know the señor?'

'Sufficiently well for him to ask me to marry him . . . Life's a switchback, isn't it? A switchback one isn't allowed to climb off. Back home, I was so depressed that suicide seemed attractive—in one month, a great friend died, my mother died, and I was made redundant. I can still see myself looking at the pack of sleeping pills I found in my mother's bedroom and wondering . . .

'It's odd how often tiny things have major consequences. I happened to see myself in the mirror and thought that I really looked like a quitter. And that so annoyed me, because I've always prided myself on being a fighter, that I shouted at the mirror that I wouldn't quit. I put on one of my favourite CDs at full volume and polished off a bottle of whisky . . . I must sound weak or stupid. Probably both?'

'Neither, Señorita. Just someone who, like most of us, has known a time when one has needed help.'

'If only everyone were that understanding . . . The really odd thing is that the next morning, when the effects of the whisky had worn off, nothing had changed. I still felt, to hell with it all. Commonsense told me to start looking for another job and that until I found one, I must conserve my redundancy money like a miser. So I decided to blow it all in one glorious Technicolor escape. I'd travel to the island of my dreams where the sun shone almost always, oranges and lemons grew in the gardens, and the world laughed. I should have remembered that the cruellest thing in life can be to find what one seeks.

'I arrived on my island; revelled in the sun, the oranges and lemons, the Technicolor life. One day I went into the newsagents to buy *The Times* and an Englishman, too precious to be true, even down to his curly golden locks, accidentally barged into me. He spent ages apologizing for his clumsiness and then invited me to have coffee with him at one of the front bars. In dirty, grey, totally unmagical London, I'd have turned the offer down flat and probably looked to see where the nearest help was if I needed it. Here, I didn't blink before accepting. It's that kind of an island. During coffee, he said he was having a party that night and would I like to go to it? Of course, I went. That's where I met Hugh.' Abruptly, she stopped speaking.

'Will you tell me about him?'

'Why d'you want to know?'

'Because if I can know him through you, I will understand that you have to be right when you say he would never willingly have touched heroin.'

'You have a Welshman's tongue of silver! All right. He was someone who added colour to even the most colourful scene, who laughed away cares, who grabbed life by the scruff and shook it. And because that's the kind of man he was, it's utterly impossible to believe he could ever have touched drugs.'

'You don't think that perhaps a little of his zest for life might have been due to an exaltation from drugs before he suffered the downside?'

'There was never any downside.' She studied him. 'You

think my judgement's too biased to be of any use, don't you?'

'Of course not . . .' he began.

'You must understand something. It's not distorted because I was in love with him. I was not in love with him.'

'But I thought you said . . .' He came to a stop.

'That I knew him sufficiently well for him to propose to me. But that also meant, sufficiently well for me not to accept.'

He was bewildered.

'He was the most wonderful company, but . . . Are you a romantic?'

'I'm not certain.'

'I am one. So when it comes to love, for me it has to be all or nothing. Hugh frankly admitted—as others had rushed to hint—that his bed hadn't been a lonely one, but he swore that if we were married, he'd never share anyone else's. I knew that it just wasn't in his character to be a hundred per cent faithful. He needed fresh conquests, not just for the usual reason, but also to confirm the fact that he directed life, unlike the ordinary person who was directed by it. Does saying all that make me sound the prime bitch?'

He was horrified by the question. 'But of course not, Señorita.'

'I'm trying to be completely honest. I have to make you understand the real Hugh and then you'll believe me when I tell you he could never have touched drugs.'

'You must understand that if that is so, then probably he was murdered.'

'That's . . .' She stopped.

'Equally impossible?'

'No one could have hated him so much. Of course there were people here who disliked him, even if they never refused to drink his champagne. The would-be Debretters who resented his wealth, the wives of retired service officers who were infuriated by his laughing at rank, the old trouts who condemned his morals because no one had ever asked them to shake a leg when they were young . . . But people don't murder for such small-minded reasons.'

He did not point out that what appeared to be small-minded to one person could appear of overwhelming importance to another. 'When I talked to Luisa, she told me that in January a man came to Ca'n Quirc who seemed to be very angry, so much so that initially she was afraid there might be a fight. Would you know anything about that incident?'

'I wasn't here in January.'

'And the señor never referred to it?'

She shook her head.

He stood. 'Señorita, permit me to thank you for your great kindness at so distressing a time.'

'If . . . if it turns out he was murdered, I hope to hell you catch the murderer.'

He wondered whether she had been completely honest when she had said she had not loved him?

'Enrique,' Dolores said, 'what is the matter?'

Alvarez looked up from the bowl of sopes Mallorquines. 'Nothing.'

'You've hardly spoken a word all evening. Something is worrying you.'

As he dug his spoon into the delicious mélange of bread, cabbage, tomatoes, garlic, onion, oil, parsley and paprika, he wondered what grasshopper was now hopping around in her mind.

'I think . . .' began Juan.

'Be quiet,' she snapped.

With typical mistiming and lack of forethought, Jaime chose this moment to try to assert his authority. 'What the

hell are you on about? Can't a man keep silent if he wants
to?'

'Would that I were married to one who had sufficient
sense to want to.'

'Here, there's no call to talk like that . . .'

She ignored him to speak to Alvarez again. 'Is it the
work?'

Alvarez swallowed his mouthful. 'Is what the work? I
don't understand.'

'Because you are determined not to.'

They ate, uneasily aware of the storm that was brewing,
but as yet unable to make out from which quarter it would
blow.

'You've been inquiring into the death of the señor from
Ca'n Quirc, haven't you?'

'So?'

'Marta is a friend of Luisa Galmes.'

He refilled his glass with wine.

'Luisa told her that the señor was always entertaining
and some of the women were so brazen they would walk
around naked.'

'Why should some people have all the luck?' Jaime asked
resentfully.

She swung round. 'Must you prove to your children that
you are not only a fool, you are a fool who suffers disgusting
lust?' She turned back. 'Luisa also said that recently the
señor has been with a very different woman—a señorita.
Is that so?'

'Yes.'

'And this señorita is young and very pretty?'

'I suppose one could say that.'

'And today you have been talking to her?'

Belatedly, he realized what was wrong. 'I can hardly
investigate without questioning everyone concerned, but if
you think . . .'

'I will tell you exactly what I think. It is because of her that you say nothing; that you dream into space.' Her voice rose. 'Why are men so stupid? Why can they never learn that a ripe pear is tastier than an unripe plum?' The expression on her handsome face was one of exasperated anger. 'Why have I invited Rosa Pons here many times if not because her husband left her a large finca with two wells, not one, that never dry out?'

'Her trouble is, she dried out a long time ago.'

That proved to be a very unwise remark to have made.

CHAPTER 8

The oldest part of the village was a warren of narrow roads and small houses which dated from times when those in power had been ready to exercise it even more rapaciously than did the tax man now so that a wise man had declared his poverty, not his wealth. A few of the houses, owned by old men and women who could often neither read nor write and found it difficult to come to terms with the modern world, still remained unreformed, but most now boasted the same amenities as more modern homes in other areas.

Alvarez stepped into the front room of Florit's house and called out. The floor was plain concrete, but on it stood a matching set of traditional Mallorquin chairs, an inlaid sideboard on which were three large pieces of Lladro, and a large refrigerator.

Florit's wife—dumpy, with a complexion tanned and seamed by sun and wind—came through the doorway, followed by a typical Mallorquin rat dog which circled Alvarez, yapping.

'I'd like a word with Florit,' he said.

She gave no response.

'Is he at home?' He waited, showing neither irritation nor impatience.

Eventually, she turned and disappeared and the dog, after one last yap, hurried after her.

Minutes later, Florit entered the room. No taller than Alvarez, both chest and shoulders were far broader; his heavy features suggested a man who would always prefer to use force to reasoned argument. 'What d'you want?' he demanded in a gravelly voice.

'To talk about the señor.'

'What señor?' When he'd been young, a peasant's only defence against authority had been assumed stupidity.

'Señor Robson.'

'He's dead. So what's there to talk about?'

'I'm hoping, quite a bit. You worked for him until recently, didn't you?'

He didn't bother to answer.

'I'd like to hear what you thought of him?'

'He was a foreigner.'

'So?'

'So he was a daft sod.'

'In any particular way?'

'Didn't want me to grow vegetables.'

'Only flowers, especially daffodils?'

Florit began to suck at his lower lip.

'I hear you grew them very successfully. Both in the señor's garden and here.'

'That's a bleeding lie. There ain't none of his bulbs here.'

'Then where did the blooms come from that you sold to the flower shop?'

Florit cursed his fate.

In this house, Alvarez thought, time had both stood still and raced ahead. When young, Florit's life had been harsh. A farmworker had been in the fields from dawn to dusk whatever the weather, had enjoyed only the most basic diet,

and had slept on straw in the loft above the animals. Then
life had begun to change with the advent of tourists and
soon their money had trickled down. For the first time in
his life, he'd not only been able to buy non-essentials, he
had dared to be seen doing so. Eventually, he had even
looked the mayor, the doctor, or the notario in the eye.
But if his lifestyle had changed beyond recognition, his
character had remained unaltered—he was still sullen,
avaricious, cunning, capable of harbouring a resentment
until he found a way of getting his own back. 'So what did
the señor say to you when he learned who'd taken the
flowers to the shop?'

'Said I'd pinched the bulbs. Called me a thief even
though them few didn't mean a bloody thing to him.'

'They obviously meant enough to sack you.'

Florit cursed.

'And that made you look stupid for letting yourself be
caught.' It was that which must have hurt. To be caught
out by a rich, stupid foreigner . . .

For Alvarez, it was one of the bitter ironies of life that his
beloved Puerto should have become a centre for drugs.
Had he had his way, those who had decriminalized the
possession of drugs for personal use would have been made
to deal with the consequences. But whoever had heard of
a people wise enough to make their politicians pay the price
of their follies?

He faced Delgado across the café table. 'Let's say, I hear
rumours from time to time.' He would have given much to
be able to prove the truth. But Delgado was smart and, so
it was rumoured, had high protection. Alvarez stared across
what had been part of the front road, but was now paved
for pedestrians, at a jetty for the use of hotel guests, from
the end of which it was safe to dive. 'I'm interested in
someone who may have been buying heroin.'

'Then I wouldn't know anything about him.'

'The name's Señor Robson.'

'Is he the guy who died from an overdose?'

'That's probably right.'

'He's not been in the market.'

'Then let's talk about a Mallorquin.'

'Does he have a name?'

'I can't remember what that is.'

'No name, no comment.'

'He's old and won't ever have used the stuff. So when he bought, he'd have stood out like a priest in a knocking shop.'

'You can't have met many priests lately.'

Alvarez was silent.

Delgado drained his glass. 'Drink up.' He signalled to a nearby waiter.

Since it had been Delgado who had suggested they drank at the front bar, and not in one two roads back where prices would be very much less, and who was now calling for refills, he surely could reasonably be expected to pay. Alvarez finished his brandy.

The waiter collected the glasses and hurried away, to return within a couple of minutes. He put two glasses down on the table, added the bill to the one already on the spike that was set in a square of polished wood.

Delgado drank. 'Just an old man who suddenly needed some shit?'

'That's the way it might have been.'

'But wasn't.'

'You're sure?'

'I'm not sure of anything like that,' he replied and laughed. He drained his glass, stood, lifted the two bills off the spike and strode off, narcisistically confident that the younger women at the other tables would be watching him because a tall, sleekly handsome man had always filled their Mediterranean daydreams.

Alvarez drank. Delgado's father still lived in an unreformed caseta and cultivated a patch of rocky ground to produce fruit and vegetables for his wife and himself. When Delgado had begun to have money to burn, he'd offered to buy his father a modern apartment so that he and his wife could live in comfort and ease. His father had replied with quiet dignity that he preferred to lead a poor life that was clean to a rich life that was dirty. It warmed Alvarez's soul to know that there were still those whose values remained untainted by the vice of money . . .

'Hullo again.'

Startled, he looked up at Honor. He hastily came to his feet. 'Good morning, Señorita.'

'For heaven's sake, make it Honor.'

She was wearing a bikini that was more modest than many. Yet there was still a lot of flesh visible and this must attract the interest of those who were of a lustful nature. She had a towel in her hand and he wished she'd wrap it around herself . . .

'It's nice to have seen you again.' She turned to leave.

He pulled himself together. 'Please sit down and have a drink.'

She turned back. 'Do you mean that?'

'Why should I not?'

'Yesterday you were charming but rather official, so maybe you still are and the invitation is really just politeness?'

'It most certainly is not.'

'Then I'm glad.' She smiled at him, sat.

He asked her what she'd like to drink. She asked for an orange juice. He called a waiter across and ordered that and another brandy for himself. She leaned her head back and shut her eyes. 'Do you know what I do each morning when I wake up? I push the shutters back and stare out at the sunshine and hope it's raining in London because that makes it so much more wonderful out here. Isn't that wicked of me?'

'Of course not.'

'But if I were a really nice person, I'd will the Londoners as much sun as I'm enjoying.' She opened her eyes and studied him. 'You're beginning to think I really am rather a nasty sort of a person.'

'I'm thinking nothing of the sort.'

'Yet . . .' Her tone subtly altered. 'Yet here I am, talking about enjoying myself only a couple of days after Hugh died. It must seem I don't care. I do. Only I've always believed that sadness is a private thing and doesn't have to be broadcast; that a person can be honestly sad and yet still enjoy life. I know that seems to be a contradiction and so you may not understand what it is I'm trying to say.'

'I'm sure I understand perfectly.'

'Then I was correct yesterday.'

'About what?'

'After you'd left, I decided that you . . .' She stopped.

The waiter put the drinks down on the table. He hurried away, his face beaded with perspiration.

'What did you decide about me?' Alvarez asked.

'I don't think I should tell you.'

'Having gone so far, if you don't, I'll suspect the worst.'

'I'd hate that! I decided you were someone who'd understand because you could always sympathize, even when the other person acted in a way you wouldn't. Am I right?'

'I should like to hope so.' Her eyes, he thought, were a blue even more beautiful than the bay.

Her glass had frosted and she began to trace a pattern with her forefinger. 'You know, it's odd but since Hugh died, I've been wondering why I didn't say "yes" when he asked me to marry him.'

'Have you come to a conclusion?'

'Only that I'll never really know why I didn't like him that extra bit. Why does one like A, but love B? I suspect that the answer has to be tinged with hypocrisy.'

'That's rather a sad conclusion.'

'But surely relationships are so often basically false?' She studied him. 'You obviously disagree.'

'I would prefer to.'

'You know, the world of today is dangerous for idealists.'

'Perhaps . . . Señorita . . .' He hastily corrected himself. 'Honor, will you tell me something?'

'If I want to.'

'Did you think the señor was unjust when he sacked the gardener?'

'Yes and no. Hugh was so honest that he viewed dishonesty much more strictly than most other people. But the loss of a few bulbs was so small a matter that . . . Frankly, when he told me what had happened, I said he must take Florit back. He wouldn't. And after a while, I could see his point. Admittedly, a few bulbs meant nothing to him, but it did show that Florit couldn't be trusted. Hugh needed above all else to be able to trust those people who were around him.'

'Why was this unusually important?'

'Because he had an image of the world that he desperately wanted to be true and he hated anything which threatened to deny that it was.'

One thing was certain—Robson had not been the idealist that she had thought him to be.

'Why are you looking like that?'

'I'm not sure how I'm looking.'

'Like someone tasting something nasty, but too polite to say so . . . Look, when one got to know Hugh well, one realized that under the smart, sophisticated surface there was someone quite different. Hugh, maybe naïvely, wanted a happy world. That's why he despised the local snobs, because snobbery has to make someone unhappy; he was so sharp on honesty and used to say that the honest man laughs longer and harder than the dishonest one; he remained pleasant and friendly when that man unexpectedly turned up and tried to be as unpleasant as possible.'

'You're talking about the visitor in January I mentioned before?'

'No, I'm not. As I told you, I wasn't here in January. I'm referring to the man who came to the house just before Hugh flew to France at the end of last month.'

'Why did the señor go to France?'

'I've no idea.'

'Was there some connection with this visitor?'

'When I said I've no idea, I mean literally just that. Hugh could be very secretive at times.'

'Did you meet this man?'

'No, just heard him. I was in the pool and a little while after a car arrived there was this shouting. But by the time I was out and dry, he'd left.'

'Then I expect you asked what it was all about?'

'On the superior male assumption that every female is devoured by curiosity? I'll have you know that I'm one female who always waits to be told because I will not pry.'

'So you've no idea who he was or why he was so angry?'

'That's right.'

'Did the señor see that caller again?'

'Sorry to be boringly repetitious, but once again, I've no idea. And that is the last question I'm going to answer. So either it's goodbye, or we talk about something happier.'

He finished his drink.

She looked across and smiled. 'So which is it to be?'

Her smile would scramble any man's brains. He called a waiter across and ordered another orange and brandy, careless of what they would cost.

Alvarez said he could just manage a third helping of Ciu-
rons. He pushed his plate across the table. Juan, who had
finished some time ago, became even more impatient. 'Can
I go out and play?'

As Dolores spooned the savoury mixture of chick peas,
onion, and garlic on to Alvarez's plate, she said: 'You know
very well you do not get down from the table until everyone's finished eating.'

'But Uncle never stops eating that stuff.'

Dolores, spoon in one hand, plate in the other, stared at
her son. 'Stuff! Stuff!'

Juan, suddenly aware of his blasphemy, sought frantic-
ally for something to say that would ease the situation.

She moved into dramatic overdrive. 'This is the thanks
I get! I slave in a kitchen that is hotter than the fires of
hell, spending my health to please my family, and what
thanks do I get? The food I serve is called stuff. Then from
now on, stuff is what they will eat at every meal.'

Juan would have had the sense to remain silent had not
Isabel kicked him on the shin and made a jeering face at
him. He said loudly: 'Jacob's mother drove us down to the
port and bought us an ice-cream. Do you know who we
saw there? Uncle at one of the front bars with a lady who
wasn't wearing anything.'

Dolores forgot her bitter complaint and stared at Alvarez.
'Mother of God, you've lost the few wits you had!'

He hurried to correct the erroneous description. It was
true that he had had a drink with a señorita, but she had
been wearing a bikini of such modest configuration that
not even a nun would have been ashamed to be seen in it
... It became obvious that neither Dolores nor Jaime
believed him. She was certain that where young women
were concerned, he was such a fool that it was more than
likely he had become enamoured of one who lacked all

sense of shame, Jaime was unwilling to relinquish the mental pictures his son had painted in his mind.

Alvarez drank. As an early Spanish philosopher had written, wine is truth, all else is a lie.

CHAPTER 9

The house lay to the north of the marshes which had, against considerable opposition from developers, been declared a nature reserve. As built, its sole purpose had been to offer shelter to beast and man and no thought had been given to style or comfort—the windows had been unglazed and only protected by solid shutters, the wood of which had warped and split; several of the rooms had lacked doors. An Englishman had bought it by lying to the elderly Mallorquin owner who was simple enough to believe all Englishmen were honest. Coming from Surbiton, the new owner had added a grand portico, an upstairs balcony with bulbous wooden pillars, and a kitchen extension with a flat roof and rendered concrete block walls. When he sold, at a great profit, he described the house as beautifully restored and for once believed he was telling the truth.

Alvarez parked in the semi-circular drive, crossed to the pretentious portico, rang the bell. The middle-aged woman, wearing a maid's apron, who opened the door was an old acquaintance and it was only after they'd discussed mutual friends that he explained the reason for his visit. She showed him into the sitting-room.

The single window—when enlarged during the reformation, part of the wall had fallen in—offered a view of the reed beds and the roof of the building which had once been a paper factory. For him, the sight of the reeds revived old memories. Soon after the family had moved to Llueso, while still a lad, he and others had often sneaked into the marshes to set traps, made from thin branches lashed together into the shape of pyramids and baited with grain, for the wild ducks. No other ducks had ever tasted as sweet as those he carried home hidden under his sweater . . . Each year, a very wealthy Arab had rented the duck shooting and his arrival had always caused so much *brouhaha* amongst the young that the village priest had felt compelled to preach a sermon on the Christian contempt for possessions. What he'd never seemed to realize was that it was not the fabulous wealth of the visitor which had caused such excitement, it had been the fact that all four of his wives had invariably been young and attractive . . .

''Morning.'

He turned. Tait stood six feet tall and not much less around the stomach. His red complexion suggested a delight in quality Riojas. 'Good morning, Señor.'

'The maid says you're some kind of a policeman, what?'

'Inspector Alvarez of the Cuerpo General de Policia.'

'Sounds impressive enough. You're here because of Hugh's death?'

'I'm afraid that that is so.'

'Damned sad business. One minute as fit as a fiddle, the next a goner. Just proves that you never can tell.'

'That is so true.'

'You know, you speak surprisingly good English for a foreigner!'

It was the first time he'd been called a foreigner in his own country. 'It is flattering to hear you say so.'

Tait failed to appreciate the possibility of irony. 'Praise where praise is due. Now then, let's start with the important things in life. What'll you drink?'

'Might I have a coñac, please; with just ice.'

'And shaken, not stirred?' When he saw that the reference was not understood, he forgivingly shrugged his shoulders.

Foreigners could not be expected to have a developed sense of humour. 'It's good to meet another brandy man,' he said as he crossed the carpeted floor to a cabinet, from which he brought a bottle and glasses. 'Went to a party the other day and asked for a horse's neck and the host didn't know what I was talking about. But then, he's a politician.' He half filled the glasses with brandy. 'I'll just go through to the kitchen for ice.' He left, to return with a chromium container.

After handing Alvarez a glass, he sat on the second arm-chair. He raised his glass. 'To a long life and a short death.' He drank with enthusiasm. 'So, now let's hear what it is you're after.'

'I understand you often played golf with the señor and so I'm hoping you'll be able to tell me about him.'

'Tell you what about him?'

'To begin with, how would you describe his character?'

'Always cheerful, always ready with a joke. Not like some of the Jeremiahs who live here and never find anything right with the world unless the stock-market's on the up and up.'

'Did he often talk about himself?'

'Wasn't that kind of a man. Can't play golf with someone who goes on about his troubles.'

'Did he often mention his wife?'

'Which one are you talking about?'

'He'd been married more than once?'

'Twice, to my knowledge. He used to say that marriage was the triumph of hope over experience. Damned witty bloke, Hugh!'

'Do you know where either his wife or ex-wife lives?'

'I got the impression the first one died. Could be wrong about that, of course. The lady wife says I get most things wrong.'

'What about his second wife?'

'She's not on this island, but that's all I can tell you about her.'

'Did he have many friends here?'

'As I always say, first define "friend". There aren't enough of us ex-pats to be able to pick and choose as much as we'd like, so we find ourselves meeting some very odd birds. Went to a cocktail party not so long ago and found myself talking to a man who said he'd voted Labour all his life.'

'But the señor knew several people he liked?'

'That's right. And then there were those whom he kept in touch with because they amused him.'

'Did he have many enemies?'

'Good God, what a question! Are you telling me he was murdered, like some people have been saying?'

'We cannot know for certain until we have the results of the post-mortem.'

'So what killed him?'

'An overdose of heroin.'

'Poppycock! Hugh never so much as touched the stuff.'

'Why are you so certain?'

'Because he was so smart and sharp.'

The door opened and a woman entered. Tait sprang to his feet and Alvarez did the same.

'Hullo, old girl,' Tait said. 'Didn't expect you back so soon. Thought you were having a chinwag with Linda.'

'When I arrived, Edith had unexpectedly turned up ten minutes before and was in full flood,' she said in a deep voice. 'That woman can't talk about anything but her grandchildren. Bloody little horrors.' She turned to Alvarez. 'Who are you?'

'Inspector Alvarez,' Tait said hurriedly, embarrassed by his failure to make the introduction. He's asking questions about poor old Hugh.'

'Señora,' said Alvarez, and briefly inclined his head.

Only slightly less rotund than her husband, her face expressed selfish determination. An ardent chaser of foxes, he decided.

As she sat on the settee, her straight skirt rode half way up her solid thighs; she made no attempt to tug it down. 'Terry, I'll have a G and T. And make it a strong one to wash away the taste of those bloody obnoxious grandchildren.' Hardly pausing for breath, she said to Alvarez: 'So someone *did* bump off Hugh!'

'We can be certain of nothing, Señora, until we have the results of the post-mortem.'

Tait said, from the far side of the room: 'The inspector seems to think the cause of death was heroin. I told him, sheer twaddle. Hugh wouldn't have touched the stuff in a month of Sundays.'

'Wouldn't he?'

'Come on, old girl, be fair.'

'I've told you more than once—only you'd never listen because he helped you control your slice—he was capable of anything.'

'You'll be giving the inspector the wrong impression.'

She made a sound that could only be described as a snort.

'You did not like him very much?' Alvarez said.

'I always kept him at arm's length.' She laughed boisterously. 'Unlike those floozies of his! But I'll say this much. He was good company, even if there was always the touch of the rotter about him.'

'Steady on,' said Tait, as he crossed to hand her a glass.

'I don't believe in sanctification through death. Half the saints would be kicked out of the calendar if the whole truth about 'em was known.'

'But he wasn't really a rotter. What upset you was his odd sense of humour.'

'Warped, more accurately.'

'In what way was his sense of humour unusual?' Alvarez asked.

'Can't explain really,' Tait answered. 'I mean, you had to know the man.'

'Doesn't the name say it all?' she asked belligerently.

'I know you've never understood why that's amusing . . .' He trailed off into silence.

Alvarez waited, but nothing more was said. 'What name were you referring to, Señora?' he asked.

'The house. Bloody stupid!'

'Not if you understand,' said her husband.

'Understand what?'

'Why he changed it. I mean, he heard the story about the oak trees. Quercus something or other is the botanical name for the evergreen oak and a quirk in English is an odd bit of behaviour.'

'You've told me that God knows how many times and I still think it's as stupidly pointless as those woodcarvings.'

Alvarez prodded the conversation along once more. 'Which woodcarvings are you talking about, Señora?'

She drained her glass. 'I'll have another. And this time, try more G with the T.'

Tait took her glass, saw Alvarez's was empty and crossed to collect his. He carried them over to the cabinet.

'Señora, you were going to tell me about the woodcarvings.'

'Nothing to tell except to say that as far as I'm concerned, they were a stupid waste of money.'

Tait returned and handed them their refilled glasses.

'Señor,' said Alvarez, 'can you tell me anything more about the carvings?'

Tait did not answer until he'd refilled his own glass and sat. 'You know you can't go into a memento shop between here and Palma without meeting the crudest of carvings of Don Quixote and Sancho Panza? Hugh decided to have carvings of them done by the finest woodcarver in the country and he put 'em on the mantelpiece in his sitting-room. When he had new visitors, he'd say: Aren't those figures wonderful? They'd take one look and reckon they were the usual rubbish, but told him yes, they were some of the most beautiful carving they'd ever seen.'

'I don't think I quite understand why the señor would wish to deceive them like that?'

'It foxed me at first, especially when I heard what they'd cost. But he explained one day. It gave him tremendous pleasure to watch his visitors, especially the more pompous ones, being hypocrites. They hadn't the taste to appreciate what they'd seen and thought the carvings were terrible, but made out they liked 'em because they didn't want to upset him.'

Perhaps, Alvarez thought, only an Englishman could truly understand all that. 'Señor, can you remember a morning in January when you were going to play golf with Señor Robson, but at the last moment he had to cancel the arrangements?'

'Can't say I do. That's a long time ago.'

'Of course you remember it,' corrected his wife. 'That's when Hugh telephoned to cancel and so you were here when Doreen called and blubbed because Tom had left her to be with that peroxide blonde.'

'By God, now I remember!' He chuckled. 'I always reckon that the lady in question must have been grievously disappointed. Never could see Tom winning medals in bed!'

'I said to Doreen that she was well shot of him, but she's a silly woman and got all excited about what the neighbours would think. As if that mattered a damn!'

She did indeed have to be a silly woman if she had chosen to come to this house for sympathy, Alvarez thought. 'The visitor arrived at the señor's house and then later both of

them left, in their own cars. I've been wondering if perhaps
they had lunched at the golf club?'

'You're smarter than you look! Quite right, that's just
what they did do. Hugh told me over the phone that he
couldn't make the game, but he'd try to eat at the club, so
I went along on the off-chance.'

'Do you remember the name of his friend?'

'You certainly ask some stiff ones!' He fiddled with his
glass. 'Something tells me it had to do with London . . . I
say, old girl, who were that couple we met in Madeira and
liked?'

'They lived in Durham and you didn't like 'em because
she said your jokes were crude.'

'Bit of a prude, wasn't she? But what was their moniker?'

'The Jekylls.'

'That's it. Hyde Park.'

'His name was Hyde Park, Señor?'

Tait roared with laughter. 'That's a good one! Just about
suits him. Only it was Hyde; just Hyde. Rum sort of cove.'

'In what way?'

'Well I'm the last person to say Hugh was a snob, but
he did like a certain *je ne sais quoi* in people and this Hyde
man was a real bangers-and-mash type.'

'Did you learn whereabouts on the island he lives?'

'Somewhere beyond Andraitx. When I learned that, I
asked him if he knew two friends of ours—Betty and Julian.
Said he didn't.'

'That was a bloody silly question,' she said.

'Why so?'

'You know what Betty thinks of cloth caps.'

'I suppose that's right . . .'

'Too much vino.'

He chuckled. 'Say what you like about Hugh, he never
ordered corriente.'

Alvarez said. 'Did you understand that Señor Hyde and Señor Robson were friends?'

'As I remember things, I began wondering if Hugh was having a quiet laugh at the Hyde man. Rather like he used to laugh at the people who praised his carvings.'

'Do you suppose Señor Hyde imagined he was being laughed at?'

'Shouldn't think so. Those kind of people aren't very wide awake.'

'Can you remember anything more about him?'

'Only that his clothes were scruffy and his car was ready for the junk yard.'

'Señor, can you suggest why anyone should have a motive for murdering Señor Robson?'

'Damned if I can!'

She said: 'Perhaps there's someone he cheated like he cheated you.'

'Steady on. No telling tales out of school.'

'I need to know what happened,' Alvarez said.

'Not this time, old boy. Sorry and all that, but there are some things one doesn't talk about.'

'Twaddle!' she said loudly. She faced Alvarez. 'My husband was playing a round of golf for a stake of a thousand pesetas. I, as I often do, went with them; exercise keeps the liver healthy. At the eighth they both sliced into the rough and I went to help my husband search and on the way saw where Hugh's ball had dropped. It was in a hollow and his only way out was to chip backwards. Yet when he made his stroke, he came straight out and almost on to the green. Obviously, he'd moved the ball after I'd gone past, not realizing I'd seen it.'

'You could have been mistaken about the lie,' protested Tait weakly.

'Don't be so ridiculous. He cheated to try to win that thousand pesetas even though it was a mere nothing to him. I've always said that behind all those smiles there was the mind of a barrow-boy.'

A few minutes later, Alvarez returned to his car. He drove back along the dirt track. Robson had picked up and the discarded, with cruel indifference, a succession of women; he'd sacked the gardener when there had been no need for such heavy-handed action; he'd amused himself by secretly laughing at people he'd treated as friends; he'd cheated in a game of golf because he had to win. Far from the thoughtful, charming man the señorita declared him to have been. But that merely went to prove the truth of the old saying, love turns a man into a fool, but makes a woman blind.

CHAPTER 10

The phone rang. 'Is that you, Enrique?' a woman asked in Mallorquin.

Alvarez couldn't identify the speaker. 'Who's that?'

'Luisa. You've got to come here.'

'What's happened?'

'The señor's house has been ransacked. Everything's all over the place. I've never seen such a terrible mess. Who could do such a terrible thing to the home of a man who's not yet in his grave?'

Luisa had not exaggerated. Every room in Ca'n Quirc now looked as if a typhoon had swept through the house.

'Are you going to be able to say if anything's missing?' he asked, as he stood in the sitting-room.

'When it's like this everywhere?' She gestured with her hands.

Cushions had been slit, the carpet dragged back, every

book had been pulled off the four shelves and dumped on the floor, the paintings had been taken down from the walls, many of the bottles that had been in the cocktail cabinet had smashed on the floor, as if an arm had swept them out the more quickly to see what lay behind them, the television, video, receiver, and hi-fi had been wrenched open, the wooden carvings of Don Quixote and Sancho Panza had been broken at the necks.

'Who could do such a thing?' she said, for the umpteenth time.

The casual thief would have taken the electronic equipment and would not have bothered about the books, the cushions, the paintings, or the carpet. This intruder had been searching for something.

'What am I to do?' she asked.

'Leave everything exactly as it is until I've checked.'

'But that doesn't seem right.'

'Nevertheless, that's how it's to be.'

He was going to have to search through the destruction, hoping to find something that would indicate who the intruder was and what he had been after. It was a task that would have daunted Hercules; compared to this, the cleansing of the Augean stables had been a pleasant afternoon's watering. 'But before I start work, I need a booster. So how about making some coffee and adding a glass of that superb coñac.'

She found the coffee machine and a tin of coffee amongst the mess in the kitchen, prepared the machine and put it on the stove. She then left, to return in less than a minute. 'The bottle of coñac was one of those that was broken.'

'Vandal!'

'But I expect there are one or two more down in the cellar. Would it be all right to get one of those?'

'The señor would undoubtedly approve.'

As he waited, he savoured the delight to come—an enjoyment that was brought to an abrupt end when she returned empty-handed and said: 'Lots of the bottles in the cellar have been broken and I can't find any coñac at all.'

He was lost for words.

The land encompassing the circle of oaks belonged to Ferrer. His was a blessed farm. His crops never failed and his wells never dried out, his sheep bore healthy twins and even triplets, his cows gave floods of milk, and his pigs farrowed without the loss of a single piglet. Inevitably there were those who suggested that in his youth he had stood within the oaks and had wished.

'I wasn't around after dark.' He was short, had forearms the size of thighs, and a barrel of a chest. For years he had been the island's stone-lifting champion, a sport borrowed from the Basques.

'So you didn't see anyone drive up to the señor's house during the night?'

'Couldn't, could I, seeing I was back in my place in the village?'

Alvarez stared at the flock of sheep and lambs in the next field. Each sheep had a bell tied around its neck and when several moved there was a sound, basically unmusical and yet music to the ears of any true countryman, that was supremely evocative.

Ferrer hawked and spat. 'You say he smashed most every bottle?'

Even the Torres Hors d'Age.'

'The silly bugger's mad.'

Ferrer's sheepdog, a direct import from Wales, bored, sidled towards the gate. Ferrer shouted and it dropped to the ground and began to pant.

'Were you around earlier in the day, keeping an eye on the sheep?' Alvarez asked.

'D'you take me for a Sunday farmer?' he replied sarcastically.

A heron lazily flapped its way up the valley, doubtless intent on raiding a goldfish pond—another introduction of the foreigners who seemed to have endless ways of wasting money.

'When you were out this morning, did you see anyone hanging around the place?'

'There weren't no one.'

'Did you happen to see a car parked on the road for any length of time?'

Ferrer thought back. 'There was one bloke watching birds. Daft bugger! What's the good of looking at birds you ain't going to eat?'

'How do you know he was bird-watching?'

'He was using a pair of binoculars, wasn't he?'

'In which direction was he looking?'

'Up at the mountains behind us.'

'Were there any special birds around?'

'What's special?'

'For the likes of them? Hawks, black vultures, bee eaters, golden orioles.'

'The bee eaters was around earlier, but they'd moved on by the time he was down there.'

'So he could have been looking at the house and not for birds?'

Ferrer considered the question for a long time. 'Maybe.'

'Did you get a good look at him?'

'Can't say I did. Didn't take no notice of him, anyways.'

'Would you know him again?'

'Shouldn't think so.'

The dog moved, Ferrer shouted; the dog settled and wagged its tail, making a brushing noise as it swept across grass that was already turning brown.

'Did you notice anything about the car—make, colour,

what its registration number was? Was it small or large, a four-wheel drive vehicle?'

'All I know is, it was green and hired.'

'How can you be sure of that?'

'Because it had the square of paper on the back window that hire cars have to have, that's how.'

A green car, make unknown, registration number unknown, possibly hired. Echoes of a white Escort. But this time not even Salas could expect him to try to trace it. His forehead was moist from sweat and he mopped it with a handkerchief. 'It's thirsty weather.'

'There's a well in the field behind.'

He wasn't that thirsty.

The secretary with the plummy voice directed him to wait. He waited, receiver to his left ear.

Salas said, too loudly for comfort: 'What the devil's going on?'

'You mean, Señor, in respect of the death of Señor Robson?'

'Being an optimist, I have—despite experience—been waiting for an interim report on your investigation. Needless to say, I have been disappointed.'

'Things have not been easy. In view of the lack of post-mortem results, there is no certainty as yet whether the death was accidental or deliberate. In view of this, I decided that the best, perhaps the only, thing to do was to discover if anyone had a motive for murdering him in order to discover if he was murdered. I realize that this is to reverse the normal sequence of events since normally one has the certainty of a murder and then searches for the motive . . .'

'Get on with it, man.'

'What I have discovered is that the señor was two-faced. He appeared to many to be a pleasant and amusing man, but in reality he was callous: a cheat, and someone who gains pleasure from another's discomfort. I believe there is a word in German for that, but just at the moment I can't remember . . .'

'Have you identified a motive for his murder?'

'Yes and no. I have identified a motive and although it might not seem a strong one, in fact, if one understands the mind of a Mallorquin one can appreciate that in reality it can be.'

'An appreciation, then, that will only come with difficulty to someone of intelligence. Nothing more concrete than this?'

'Well I . . . I hesitate to say so, Señor, but I have a feeling about this case.'

'It is to be regretted that your hesitation was not more pronounced.'

'I am becoming more and more convinced that unless the widest possible inquiries are made, we may well miss the truth. As Llogut wrote, the truth often hides within the truths. The señor was not the man that he wished the world to believe him, so what more likely than that the true motive for his murder will be hidden deep? If this is so, we will have to search far and wide, remembering that what appears to be simple will in truth be complicated . . .'

'Left to you, it will be a blasted cat's cradle. Restrict your investigation to the facts and let me have a written report by the end of the week.'

'By the end of this week, Señor?' Alvarez asked in amazement.

'That's right.' The connection was cut.

He sighed. If cases with which he was concerned did occasionally tend to become complicated, the fault could often be traced to Salas's Madrileño penchant for rush. Time spent in contemplation was never wasted. To hurry was so often to stumble . . . Sweet Mary, but he'd just stumbled badly! He'd forgotten to mention the break-in.

He phoned and the plum-voiced secretary put him through to Salas.

'What the devil is it now?'

'Señor, we were cut off before I had a chance to report what happened yesterday. There was a man on the Laraix road watching birds . . .'

'Are you under the mistaken impression that not only am I interested in birds, I have nothing better to do than to discuss them?'

'The important thing is, I don't think he was watching birds.'

'Then no doubt you now wish to regale me with information concerning a second man who was not sunbathing?'

'I think he was probably casing Señor Robson's house.'

'Have you anything approaching a reason for such a belief?'

'The fact that the señor's house was broken into and ransacked.'

Salas, allowing his anger to get the better of him, shouted: 'Goddamnit, you haven't even learned not to make a report upside down and inside out!' He managed to speak more calmly. 'What's been stolen?'

'Everything's in such a mess, it's virtually impossible to say. But what is significant is what has not been stolen.'

'But of course! To you, what has not taken place has always to be of much more importance than what has.'

'Señor, along with so much else, the television and video have not been taken but have been smashed open and left. This was not an ordinary thief, it was a man searching for something. And searching so exhaustively and with such destruction that it must be of very great value. Then here surely has to be the true motive for the señor's death. And proof that he was murdered and did not die accidentally.'

'I suppose it is very naïve of me still to be surprised that you cannot begin to distinguish between theory and fact.

It has not occurred to you that if one accepts that the señor died from heroin poisoning, it is obvious that he had a source? This means, other addicts will have known about his addiction. And it is probably one of those who ransacked the house, searching for the cache of heroin he believed hidden in it.'

'Naturally, I did consider the possibility, Señor. And I suppose the fact that the house was turned over so completely does tend to suggest the frenzy of a man desperate for his next fix, but I have the feeling that this is the wrong explanation . . .'

The line went dead. As he replaced the receiver, he realized that in his enthusiasm to explain, he'd again made the mistake of talking about his instinctive feelings.

CHAPTER 11

The solicitor rang first. He had done work for Señor Robson, in the course of which he'd advised him that it was much in his interests to make a Spanish will before he bought property because if he failed to do so, and relied on an English will, then on his death the state could be relied upon to get their hands on much of the estate.

'Do you have a copy of his will?'

'Indeed. You wish to know the details?'

The will proved to be brief and concise. Robson left everything he possessed in Spain to his wife.

'Does he name her?'

'No. Naturally, I told him that he should. But, as I clearly remember, he said that he didn't want the additional expense of changing his will every time he changed his wife. A somewhat unusual attitude, even for a foreigner.'

'If he didn't name her or give an address, how can you contact her?'

'I can't. Which is why I'm hoping you can help me.'

'Not for the moment, but with a bit of luck maybe later on. Have you any idea what size the estate will be?'

'There's the house, which is worth a great deal of money, but beyond that I have no information. Once again, I'd be grateful for any help.'

After the call was over, Alvarez leaned back in the chair. The two most common motives for murder were love and money; of the two, money was the stronger (it lasted longer). Could Robson's second wife have learned that her husband was intending to divorce her, which would have cut her out of his will?

The bank phoned later that morning.

'Alejandro here, Enrique. I've just heard from Head Office; they've authorized me to cooperate.'

'That's good news.'

'I don't think that what I can tell you will be of as much help as you're probably hoping. Like all rich foreigners, Señor Robson kept all his capital outside Spain and only brought in enough for his running expenses.'

'But you'll know where the money from abroad came from?'

'The Banque d'Anguette in Geneva.'

'If I ask them for their help, d'you think they'll give it to me?'

'If you can prove that there's been a criminal offence committed and the señor's financial affairs are an essential part of your investigation, you should be able to gain their cooperation.'

'I can't do that as yet.'

'Then your other hope is to obtain the assent of the beneficiaries to your being given the facts and figures.'

'There's just the wife and I don't know how to get hold of her.'

'Life was never meant to be easy . . . By the way, I don't know if it's of any interest to you, but he did deposit a small strong-box with us.'

'It could be, I suppose. I'll be along later.'

It felt and sounded as if it contained something small and loose.

'When did he leave this with you?' Alvarez asked.

The manager, small, dumpy, prematurely bald, wearing large glasses which gave him an owl-like appearance, consulted a ledger. 'At the beginning of this month; on the fifth.'

'I suppose you've no idea what's inside?'

'Of course not.'

'Do you have a key somewhere which we could try to see if it fits?'

'You have a queer idea about how banks go about their business.'

'Suppose I say I'd like to take it away and have it opened?'

'I was told I could cooperate fully. So provided you sign a receipt which specifically states you received the box locked, I'm prepared to hand it over.'

Alvarez returned to his car and drove half way up the hill around which the village was built and parked by one of the Stations of the Cross which lined the road. He crossed to a flight of stone steps, descended these, entered the house at their foot and called out. After a while, an old woman, with a face so creased that at first sight it appeared deformed, appeared. He said he wanted a word with Andrés.

Because the house was built on the side of the hill, the view encompassed the Cala Roig valley, Llueso Bay, and a distant skyline of Playa Neuva; foreigners, provided they had never experienced the level of noise in the summer, would have paid a great deal for a house in such a situation. Ocaña was ignoring the view and watching television. Older than his wife by two years, ironically his facial skin had remained supple so that he looked several years younger. He screwed up his eyes as he stared at Alvarez.

She shouted: 'It's Enrique. Dolores's cousin.' When he seemed to find the words meaningless, she said to Alvarez: 'It's one of his bad days.'

For several more seconds, Ocaña continued to stare blankly at him, then suddenly he nodded, grinned to show uneven, broken teeth, and greeted him coherently.

'I've come to ask you to do a little job for me.'

Ocaña shook his head. 'Me fingers is aching something terrible.'

'Can't the doctors help?'

'Never done me no good.'

'Because you won't take the medicine they give you,' she shouted.

He ignored her.

Alvarez showed him the strong-box. 'I need to find out what's inside and there's no key.'

'I don't do nothing these days.'

'This is strictly legal.'

Ocaña rubbed the side of his nose, stared across at his wife who remained in the doorway. After a while, he held out his hands for the box. He rested it on his lap, peered at the lock, his eyes half screwed up. 'You mean you can't open this?'

'That's right.'

'Always were bloody useless!' He turned to his wife. 'Get the wires out.'

She left. When she returned, she came into the room to hand him a canvas roll. He unwound this and from one of

the many compartments brought out a skeleton key which
looked rather like a dentist's probe. He inserted this in the
lock and manipulated it with a delicate ease which seemed
to belie his rheumatism. The lock clicked open.

'You've not lost any of your skills!' Alvarez said admir-
ingly. He took the box and opened the lid. Inside was a
single videotape, the back of its case labelled 'Son of
Pecksniff'.

He drove home to find the house locked and let himself
in, not without a mental backward glance to the days when
theft had been so unknown that one had left the key of the
outside door in the lock to show that no one was at home.
In the dining-room, he switched on the TV and video,
inserted the tape. There was no picture. He scratched his
head, wondering what was the point of keeping a blank
tape in the bank, then remembered that he'd not changed
the channel on the TV. He pressed the appropriate button
on the remote control, glad that Juan was not present to
comment sarcastically on his electronic incompetence. A
moment later, he was even gladder. The camerawork was
poor, mainly due to lighting, but there was not the slightest
doubt that the couple were performing intricate variations
on an ancient theme . . .

'What are you doing back here at this time of the day?
Are you ill?' Dolores asked from the doorway, her voice
filled with sudden, sharp concern.

He started. 'I didn't hear you come in.'

She entered the room and for the first time looked at the
screen. Her expression changed from concern to bewilderment, from bewilderment to outrage. 'What are you watching?' she asked in a furious, ice-laden voice.

'Santa María!' He grabbed the remote control and in his
panic pressed the fast forward button. The movements of
the couple became breathtaking. Then he found and
depressed the stop button.

'That you should bring such disgusting filth into my house!' This was one of her actress manqué moments. 'That I should find my own cousin has tastes which were born in the gutter! That you sneak into my house to indulge in your perverted pleasures!'

'I had to watch it,' he protested.

'Are you, then, beyond all redemption?'

'You don't understand. It's to do with the case.'

'And you think me fool enough to accept such nonsense?' She marched through to the kitchen, head held high.

He was not going to be allowed to forget this in a hurry, he thought gloomily, as he ejected the tape, then replaced it in its cover.

He was correct. When lunch was finally served, the soup was almost cold, the pork undercooked and the cauliflower overcooked, the bananas were brown and squashy, the almonds had not been toasted. Even worse, the bottle of wine on the table was only half full and the sideboard proved to be empty of any replacements.

Later, when she was washing up in the kitchen amidst a great deal of banging, Jaime said angrily: 'You're a silly bastard!' What riled him more than anything was the fact that he had had to suffer Dolores's anger even though he'd not seen the tape.

When pornographic tapes could be hired without the slightest trouble, when many newsagents and even some of the supermarkets sold them, why should Robson have bothered to keep this tape in the bank? Remembering the other's odd, cruel sense of humour, it seemed possible that the title on the cover might suggest the answer—but it meant nothing to him. Which left him to fall back on the obvious. The poor quality of the lighting and the way the figures had frequently moved out of the centre of focus suggested that either the cameraman had been a rank amateur or the camera had been fixed. Blackmail? He must view the rest of the tape to see if he could learn anything more from it.

As he walked up to the front door of the bungalow, he suffered the prickles of tension. That he did so, he assured himself, was all Dolores's fault. But for her, Honor would merely have been a young and attractive woman whom he had met through the case and for whom he felt considerable sympathy; nothing more. But Dolores insisted on seeing smoke where there was no fire, and never had been, and so now, as he rang the bell, he remembered all she'd said and he could not stop himself wondering . . .

'Shan't be a moment. Just putting on some clothes.'

Resolutely, he steered his thoughts away from the path along which they threatened to tread and concentrated on the joys of harvesting sweet peppers.

She opened the door. 'What fun to find it's you! Sorry to have kept you waiting, but I've been sunbathing in the back garden.' She studied him. 'You're looking very serious. I hope that doesn't mean more bad news?'

'Not at all.'

'Thank God for that—I've had about all I can stand. Come on through to the other room and have a drink. There's anything you'd like so long as that's gin, brandy, wine, or beer.'

He asked for a brandy. She served him that and gave herself an apple juice, sat in the second chair. 'As a matter of fact, I was going to get in touch with you.' She stared down at the glass in her hand. 'I was wondering if you'd any idea yet when . . .' She trailed off into silence.

'You want to know when the funeral will be?' he said softly.

She nodded.

'I am very sorry, but permission has not yet been given. The moment it is, I will tell you.'

'You're terribly kind.'

'It's the very least I can do.'

'It's so much more. I wonder if you've any idea how much you've helped me? You could have been rudely insensitive, instead of which you've been more like a friend than detective. When I've been seeing the world in black, you've been around to paint the corners white . . . Damnit, I can distinctly remember telling you that I believed grief should be private, yet here I am, all but crying on your shoulder. Enough of me. Let's move on to you. What's brought you here; not all business, I hope?'

He admired her more than ever for the way in which she conquered grief.

'I have been speaking to the solicitor who handled the señor's legal affairs and he's told me that the señor made a very simple will in which he has left everything to his wife. Unfortunately, it seems he has left no record of his wife's name or address or even, for that much, anything which says for certain whether she is still his legal wife— after all, he did speak to you about divorce. Before the solicitor can act in his estate, he naturally has to identify the wife and have a word with her and he's asked me if I can help him. I thought that perhaps you would know?'

'He was certainly married up to the time when he proposed to me.' She was silent for a while, then said: 'I don't think it could have been a happy marriage; not from the way he spoke about it—joking, but not joking, if you know what I mean? He told me once that her name was Penelope, but that it was difficult to think of anyone less likely to spend ten years making and unpicking a robe to keep her suitors at bay. Presumably, she wasn't as faithful as she could have been.'

'Did he ever mention where she lives?'

'It was her house, so she stayed on there after they

separated. The nearest town or village—I'm not certain which—was somewhere near Eckinstone, in Kent.'

'Did he ever mention his first wife?'

'Only to say that she died soon after they were married and when she was very young. You know . . . I've sometimes wondered if his attitude to life really stemmed from tragedy. If they were very happy together and she died suddenly, he must have been grief stricken. Grief can turn people very cynical.'

She was the most loyal of defenders; if she could find even the hint of a reason for closing her eyes, she closed them.

'For some people, life is all fun,' said Jaime, as the tape came to an end.

Alvarez crossed to the video, ejected the tape, carried it upstairs and put it in the strong-box in his bedroom. Dolores, Juan, and Isabel were not due back for at least another hour, but life had recently taught him that there were an endless number of jokers in the pack.

When he returned downstairs, there was a three-parts full bottle of Soberano and two glasses on the table. 'I found out where she hid the booze,' Jamie said proudly.

Alvarez filled a tumbler, added ice, drank. Who was the woman in the tape, who the man? Surely the tape had to be intimately connected (what description could be more suitable) with the murder—he no longer conceived accidental death to be an option—of Robson?

CHAPTER 12

The urbanizacíon lay in a shallow valley, the floor of which had always been more stone than soil; even olive trees had had to struggle to survive. The land had originally been bought by a developer with an unusual ambition—to create an up-market enclave that would attract up-market residents, which would raise the tone of the island. As usually happened, profitable idealism proved to be a disastrous idea. Half way through building the roads and installing electricity and water points on each plot—as demanded by the regulations—he had had to petition for bankruptcy. The next developer had been a down-to-earth man who concentrated on essentials. He had subdivided the plots and sold to anyone who had the money to buy.

Ca Na Naranja—there was one sad orange tree—was at the end of a spur road. It was small, boxy, and in obvious need of decoration. A far cry from Ca'n Quirc, Alvarez thought as he pressed the bell which had, incredibly, been labelled 'Ring-a-ding'.

The door was opened by a man he recognized as Hyde from the description Luisa had given him. The light blue eyes met his only for a second, then flicked away. He introduced himself.

Hyde tried, and failed, to appear nonchalantly unconcerned. 'How can I help you, then?'

'I would like to ask you one or two questions.'

'Well, I don't know. I mean, we're just on our way out. Drinks and grub with some friends.'

Alvarez waited patiently.

'I suppose that . . . You'd better come on in.'

The interior of the bungalow was in a better state of

decoration and repair than the exterior, but not by much.

There was a call from beyond the sitting-room. 'Who is it?'

'A policeman,' Hyde shouted back.

The woman who hurried in had heavily permed, blonde hair, used too much make-up, and dressed as if many years younger than she obviously was. 'What's up? Why's a policeman come here?' It was immediately apparent that she possessed the spirit of aggression which her husband lacked.

'I don't know.' Hyde risked the briefest of glances at Alvarez before he stared through the window at a century plant. He cleared his throat. 'Best sit down.' His wife joined him on the settee whose faded cover had been heavily patched in one corner. He fiddled with one of the buttons on his open neck shirt. 'So what is this all about?' he asked, his voice rising from nervousness.

'I understand you knew Señor Robson?'

'What if we did?' she snapped.

'Then I have a few questions to ask your husband, Señora. Obviously, you have heard that he died almost a week ago?'

'It was in the local rag.'

'An investigation into his death has shown that it may well not have been an accident; it is probable that he was murdered.'

'Hardly surprising!'

'For God's sake don't talk like that,' Hyde said urgently.

'I always talk as I find.' She faced Alvarez. 'He was no friend of ours.'

'You are saying that you did not like him?'

'You can't fool me with airs and graces. But you can always fool him.' She jerked her head in the direction of her husband. 'Talk like you own the world and that's why you want to do him a good turn and you'll fool him into buying Buckingham Palace.'

'How was I to know?' Hyde asked.

'By listening to me.'

Alvarez was surprised by her continuing aggressiveness; no Mallorquin woman would ever have spoken like that in front of a stranger.

Hyde said: 'But when he . . .'

'Didn't I tell you not to hand over cash because if anything went wrong, you'd lose it?'

'But you were getting so worried because we had to find more money . . .'

'Find it, not lose it.'

'I . . . I didn't think we possibly could.'

'Because you wouldn't recognize a thief even if you found him lifting your wallet out of your pocket.'

'I did talk to you about it and you said to go ahead . . .'

'So now it's all my fault?'

His brief self-defence crumbled. He stared down at the floor just beyond the toes of his scuffed sandals.

Alvarez said: 'You had a business deal with the señor?'

Unsurprisingly, it was she who answered him. 'A business swindle.'

'Why do you say that?'

'Because he took us for ten thousand quid.'

'How did this happen?'

'My husband would rush to trust Judas.'

She spoke with rapidly increasing bitterness. Back home, her husband had owned a small estate agency in an outer London suburb. He'd been completely honest and had given all his clients square deals, but when the building societies had created chains of offices they'd cut into his business and when the recession had brought sales of houses almost to a standstill, he'd become financially troubled. Mental stress had brought on a heart attack. The doctor had described it as only a mild one, but she'd been terrified that she was going to lose him . . .

Alvarez was surprised by the deep emotional feeling with which she expressed her fears. Until then, he'd placed her as a loud, pugnacious woman, capable of domineering but not of loving. He should have remembered. Love didn't have to be rose-petalled.

She continued speaking, her gaze unfocused, her tone far less strident. The specialist had assured them that if her husband was sensible, he could return to leading a normal life. But how could he, when his business was on its last legs? That was when they'd heard of a young man who, miraculously, wanted to buy an estate agency in their area . . .

Many years previously, they'd spent their honeymoon in Mallorca and so the island had always held a special place in their hearts. Life on a Mediterranean island would be so much slower and less stressful than in England. Without bothering to check if conditions had changed since their honeymoon, they'd moved out to find the good life that memories told them was waiting. Reality had proved their memories to be poor soothsayers. The price of everything, and in particular of houses, had risen out of all recognition. And because so much of their capital had had to be invested to provide an income, they'd not been able to buy their dream house overlooking the sea, but had had to settle for this small, mean bungalow . . .

The cost of living had continued to rise so quickly that the official rate of inflation became a bad joke. The pound had fallen against the peseta, interest rates in the UK had dropped. Like many other expatriates, they'd seen their standard of living slowly, then more quickly, deteriorate . . .

They'd unexpectedly been invited to a cocktail party by a couple from the toffee-nosed brigade—people who usually had difficulty even in saying good morning. At the party, they'd met Robson. He'd been very interested to learn—after the fourth or fifth champagne, one did tend to exchange confidences—that her husband had owned and run an estate agency. Before they'd left, Robson had suggested lunch at a little fish restaurant he knew in Palma. They'd been surprised and flattered—he was obviously very wealthy and they weren't used to his like being friendly, because even in a small expatriate community, accent or wealth counted for much. At the luncheon, he'd talked about a possible property development in which he was considering becoming interested. Her husband, wanting to repay the kindness, had ventured to express his professional judgement, which was that it was not the time to contemplate such an investment since even the Germans were buying less. Robson had been amused by that. Markets in any commodity, he'd said, were controlled by the lemming syndrome. Let one lemming jump off a cliff and almost all the rest would follow suit. But there'd be a few with more intelligence and they wouldn't jump because when there was so much less to share, each one's share became greater. Housing was deep in the doldrums and prices were being slashed without results, so everyone was convinced that the market was dead and only a complete fool would dream of building new houses. A complete fool or a complete savant. Every slump had to bottom out, just as every boom had to burst. So what better time to start building than when the lemmings had talked the market down to its bottom level? It would be the rich buyer who would show up first and he would demand a luxurious house on a dream site. Robson had known of a stretch of coastline that would provide sites to please even a Rothschild, the owner of which was willing to sell. But there was a problem. Some slow-witted idealist had slapped a conservation order on all the land . . . The next move was obvious, but this had to be made by someone who had a low profile—unlike himself—who knew his way around, and who had learned to judge when an official with the necessary power would, with the aid of a discreet brown envelope, become practically sympathetic. So would her husband like to become a partner in the venture and handle the often delicate task of persuading people where their true interests lay? He'd jumped at the chance, never bothering to talk it over with her . . .

'But I did,' Hyde protested.

'Not the ten thousand pounds, you didn't.'

'But I couldn't hope to become a partner without putting up some money.'

'That's not how he talked to begin with. If he had, I'd have said he could forget the idea. Him with all his money, calling on you to pay up. There had to be something fishy in that, as you'd have realized if you'd managed to keep any of your wits about you.'

'Why should I have expected there was anything wrong . . .'

Alvarez listened to an argument that must have been repeated over and over again. Eventually, it petered out as Hyde lost the spirit to reply to his wife's angry criticisms. She resumed her story. Her husband had worked at the job. No linguist, he'd attended Spanish lessons so that he could speak just a little Spanish to the people he dealt with; he'd wined and dined them; he'd used his expert judgement, largely gained from doing work for the town hall at home, to decide when to hint at brown envelopes. And every penny he'd spent had been provided by him because Robson had carefully explained how necessary it was for him to appear totally disengaged from the nuts and bolts of the wheeler-dealering . . . Everything had been going along smoothly and it had seemed the conservation order would be overturned when suddenly the whole scheme blew up. No one knew why. Her husband had gone along to Robson to ask for a refund of all the money he'd paid out. Robson had expressed surprise at the request. Surely her husband had known all along that there had to be the risk of the scheme's not going through and had, by becoming a partner, accepted such risk? It was, he had said with that wide smile of his, a poor gambler who tried to welsh.

Hyde said, his voice high: 'I begged him to repay the money; I told him now I wasn't going to get any income out of the business, I just had to have the money back to earn interest. Without it, I didn't think we could make both ends meet. He refused to repay me a penny. That's when we had such trouble with the foundations of this place and the builder estimated it was going to cost anywhere between half a million and a million and a half to put everything right, but if we didn't the place could become uninhabitable ... I was so desperate that I drove to Llueso to see him, even though he'd made it clear he didn't want anything more to do with me because I was no further use to him. It was the first time I'd seen his house. It was worth a hundred million if it was worth a peseta, even with prices low. And there was a new Mercedes outside. When I saw all that and thought about his refusing to repay me the ten thousand pounds, and how little it would mean to him and how much to us, I lost my temper.'

Had the circumstances not affected him so desperately, the thought of him losing his temper would have been amusing.

'This trip to his house was in January?' asked Alvarez.

'Sometime like that.'

'And later on the señor took you to his golf club for lunch?'

'How ... how d'you know that?'

'Your visit to the house was remembered by the maid and to the club by Señor Tait.'

'That man! Acted friendly, but all the time he was looking down his nose at me.'

'Presumably you tried once more to persuade the señor to repay you?'

'I even offered to settle for half; said that as we had been partners, wouldn't he pay me for his share of the loss? You're not going to believe this, he just laughed and told me that experience always cost and so I owed him that five thousand for tuition.'

'Did his attitude anger you?'

'What d'you think it did? Seeing him smiling and mocking me, knowing how desperately I needed the money. I could have . . .' He stopped suddenly.

'Killed him?'

His wife spoke with fresh aggression. 'We've shed no tears because he's dead. But that doesn't mean we had anything to do with his death. We didn't.'

It was difficult to imagine that Hyde would wreak revenge by murder; but quite easy to believe that she might do so.

Alvarez spoke to Salas over the phone. 'I went to the bank and secured the strong-box that Señor Robson had deposited there at the beginning of the month. It contained a videotape which I played at home. Judging by the poor quality of the images, it was almost certainly made unprofessionally.'

'Is it really of any consequence how it was made?'

'In this case, yes, Señor, it is.'

'Why? What's the tape about?'

'A man and a woman.'

'What kind of an answer is that supposed to be? Who are they, what are they doing?'

'Having sex.'

There was a long pause. 'I find it disturbingly extraordinary that you cannot conduct an investigation without introducing a strong element of pornography.'

'Señor, I cannot be blamed . . .'

'Is the man Señor Robson?'

'No, he isn't.'

'Then who is he?'

'I do not know.'

'Who is the woman?'

'I don't know her identity either, Señor.'

'Your knowledge is, as usual, severely restricted.'

'I think it must be significant that the tape was being held in the security of the bank. And one has to remember how the señor's home was ransacked by someone obviously searching for something of great importance. I'd say that this tape was being used to blackmail. If the señor was blackmailing someone, we have the motive for his murder.'

'Do I have to remind you yet again that there is no certainty his death was murder?'

'But the motive of blackmail must surely remove any doubts?'

'Must you confute all logic by supposing certain facts to be true, drawing a deduction from this supposition, and then using that deduction to confirm the truth of the original facts? . . . Is that all you have to report?'

'There is one more thing, Señor. I have managed to find out where the señor's second wife lives. Since she's the sole beneficiary under his will, it is clearly very important to question her.'

'Of course.'

'Then I'll make arrangements to interview her . . .'

'Where does she live?'

'In or near a village called Eckinstone.'

'Is that on this island?'

'It's in Kent, England.'

'Just as I thought! You were hoping to sneak away on one of your damned walkabouts!'

'But as you've agreed, someone must question the señora . . .'

'Which is why you will draw up a list of the questions that need to be put to her and I will send this to the police in England and ask them to ascertain the answers. See that the list is on my desk by tomorrow morning.' He rang off.

Tomorrow morning? If there were one lesson that every man was forced to learn, Alvarez thought, it was that life offered more brickbats than bouquets.

CHAPTER 13

Detective-Constable Barnes raised the collar of his oilskin coat, left the car, and hurried across the drive to the porch of the large Queen Anne house. Several drops of rain which had avoided his collar slid down his neck and reached the small of his back. As he rang the bell, he cursed the weather, his detective-inspector, and his stomach, which was complaining merely because he'd eaten several Scotch pancakes with maple syrup after the eggs and bacon.

The door was opened by a woman. He said: 'Mrs Robson? My name is Detective-Constable Barnes, local CID.'

'Do come in from the rain.'

He stepped into a hall on the far wall of which hung four stag heads with many points. They went well with her tweed suit, rope of pearls, and huntin', shootin', and fishin' tone of voice. 'I'd like a word with you, if I may?'

She seemed neither surprised nor curious. 'Of course. Put your coat over there.'

He hung it on a tall, six-prong mahogany coatstand, the like of which he had not seen for a long time.

'We'll go through to the blue room.'

He followed her into the very large room, confusingly more green than blue, which contained furniture that would have paid his wages for many years.

'Please sit down.'

He gingerly lowered himself on to a chair that had elegantly curved, but spindly legs. It felt surprisingly steady once he was seated.

'Now, what do you want to have a word about, Constable?'

Abruptly, and for the first time in ages, he remembered the schoolmistress who, when he'd been nine or ten, had tried to teach him maths. It was not Mrs Robson's appearance which triggered this memory, but her air of calm, confident, complete self-possession. 'I'm here at the request of the Spanish police in Mallorca.'

'Presumably, following the death of my husband?'

He was slightly surprised at the calm way in which she'd said that, even though the request had mentioned the fact that she and her husband had been separated for some time. 'I'm very sorry about that.'

'Thank you.'

Apparently as cool as a cucumber. But he noticed that she had begun to fidget with the edge of her chain. 'Would you mind telling me how you heard about his death?'

'I have friends who have a holiday home on the island and spend several weeks there each year. They phoned and told me.'

'Did they also mention . . .' He paused, to assemble his words more carefully.

'They said they'd heard the rumour that the circumstances of his death were unusual. I presume that this was one rumour that was fact since you are here now?'

'Yes.'

'He was murdered?'

'I understand that that has still to be determined. All that can be said so far is that he probably died from an overdose of heroin.'

'He would never knowingly have touched such poison.'

'Mrs Robson, when did you last see your husband?'

'When we separated, a few years ago.'

'You've not visited him on the island?'

'I have not.'

'Can you suggest who might have wished to kill him?'

'Not specifically . . . I presume that one reason for your being here now is to determine whether perhaps I had both reason and opportunity?'

The casual way in which she named herself as a possible suspect flummoxed him. He hurriedly collected his thoughts together. 'You could hardly have done so if you've never been to the island.'

'Which means you must be wondering if that is a lie.'

He felt the interview slipping away from his control. 'Is it?' he asked weakly.

'As a matter of fact, no, it isn't.'

Ironically, the firm denial made him think that possibly it was. 'You said you couldn't suggest any specific reason why someone might have a motive for killing your husband. That suggests that perhaps you think there might have been a general reason?'

'I don't know that I intended any such inference, but it's not inaccurate. I imagine that anyone who had the misfortune to learn what was his true character could well have wished him dead.'

He wondered what exactly she meant by that?

'I've not made myself clear? My husband, Constable, possessed more charm than it was right for any mortal to enjoy. Charm distorts and blinds. My father understood that which is why, had he lived long enough, he would have called me a fool.'

He'd never met a woman so obviously less of a fool.

'When he died, he left me a fortune and a letter in which he advised me on two things—how best to defend the fortune against the depredations of the Inland Revenue and the advances of avaricious men. My success with the former has been far greater than my success with the latter.'

'Mr Robson was an avaricious man?'

'Avarice comes in more than one guise. However, it must surely be obvious that it was not my sparkling beauty which attracted him?'

What the hell kind of answer was he supposed to make to this? In any case, she might not be a pin-up, but her calm self-possession held its own attraction.

'My father's influence, since he was a very strong-willed man, was not entirely dissipated. After Hugh proposed to me I decided, even though the decision briefly made me hate myself for a traitor, to hire a private detective to investigate, in so far as that was possible, his previous life. Then, with the perverted logic with which one returns to peace with oneself at such times, I convinced myself that my real motive was to prove once and for all that he was the charming, upright, honest person he presented himself to be.

'Some three weeks after I'd briefed the detective—I was surprised what a pleasant man he was—he handed me his report. I read it with disbelief and anger—anger directed at the detective, not Hugh, of course. As I said earlier, charm distorts and blinds.'

'Do you have that report?'

'Having read it through and sworn to myself that it was a tissue of monstrous lies, I tore it up and burned it.'

'Do you remember the details?'

'And if I do, why should they interest you?'

'They might contain some detail which would help the investigation.'

'They would also confirm how wilfully blind I was when I refused to believe them.'

'Everything you tell me will be held in the strictest confidence.'

'Yet a confidence to which, of necessity, many will be a party. I am a secretive person and dislike exposing myself. But then I suppose you have to deal so often with emotional stupidity that you become like a doctor, no longer astonished, perhaps not even censorious?'

He'd never compared himself to a doctor.

'I do remember most of what the report said, perhaps because I was so determined to forget every single detail.' She folded her hands in her lap. She spoke crisply and without any discernible emotion. 'Hugh claimed that he'd been born to small farmers in Herefordshire. This was the first of innumerable fictions. I've occasionally wondered why he lied about even this and have concluded that he imagined the rural touch would strike a chord in the heart of every true Englishman. In fact, he was born out of wedlock—before that became fashionable—in Lewisham. No doubt he reckoned that Lewisham would fail to strike a welcome chord in anyone.

'When he was fifteen, he was found guilty of theft, but his young age helped him to escape any condign punishment. The incident must have taught him to be more careful in future because he was never again in trouble with the law.

'He married when he was twenty-one. Her name was Libby and her parents had recently died in an aeroplane crash. From them, she'd inherited sufficient capital that meant, if carefully managed, she would be financially secure. The marriage lasted the five years that it took him to relieve her of all she possessed. At this point, he deserted

her, leaving her with a daughter, a house so heavily mort-
gaged it had to be repossessed, and an overdraft at the
bank. Small wonder that she suffered the most severe
depression and became an alcoholic and a drug addict.

'Hugh disappeared for a few years, to reappear as a property developer. Obviously an occupation that is the ideal
vehicle for a man with a silver tongue and no scruples. He
became wealthy, then sold out when property was still in
favour—Canary Wharf was an eagle, not an albatross—
and became even wealthier. We met soon afterwards.'

'Having read all this, you dismissed it completely?'

'As I said, I tried to, but the bad is always so much
stronger than the good. There was that corner of my mind
which wondered.'

'So did you ever question him about the past?'

'Have you ever done something, the doing of which
makes you mentally squirm? I asked him about his first
marriage and why it had broken up, making it sound no
more than the reasonable curiosity a second wife-to-be
might be expected to show.'

'What did he say about it?'

'He only discovered that Libby was an alcoholic after
they were married. He then did everything in his power to
persuade her to overcome her addiction and hoped that the
birth of their daughter would provide a sufficiently strong
incentive, but it didn't. Things worsened and her judgement became so hopeless that, despite everything he could
do, she lost or was swindled out of all her money. In the
end, it all became too much and he left her but, determined
to give his daughter a better life, he made an arrangement
for a family to look after the daughter until he could set up
a home for the two of them. When he tried to persuade
Libby that their daughter's future had to be with him, she
became hysterical and accused him of trying to kidnap their
daughter. It seemed that a court order was the only way

forward, but he'd no sooner consulted solicitors than she disappeared with her daughter. He tried and tried to find them, but failed. Some years later, he obtained a divorce.'

'Did you think he was telling the truth and the detective's report was wrong?'

'Of course. His silver tongue would have persuaded Polyphemus to buy binoculars. I cursed myself for ever having begun to doubt him and impatiently proposed an earlier wedding date.

'In the event, my father proved to be both right and wrong—which would have annoyed him immensely since he hated ambiguity. He was correct in believing men would wish to marry me for reasons other than my looks, he was wrong to assume that their true motives would always be financial. Hugh was richer than I. But what I had to offer him was something he desperately wanted—background and a social poise so strong that it would be obvious he always acted from choice, not ignorance. Ironically, he could not see that the age of the common man had often turned a social solecism into an asset.

'For me, marriage is a bond of loyalty as well as of love. So there were times when I should have been suspicious, but chose not to be. This made him so contemptuous of me that he became careless and I couldn't avoid knowing that he'd bought a flat in Brakenose Street, in Chelsea, and entertained women there. I faced him with the fact and told him he'd killed our marriage. He laughed, called me a melodramatic ninny, and added that marriage to me had become as exciting as—the exact simile is immaterial. He said he'd been intending to leave me anyway. I'm certain this was one more lie. It's not that he still had any affection for me—always presuming he once had had perhaps just a little—but he revelled in the social life I provided and he would have wished to carry on as we had been. However, he had to hurt me because of the cruel streak in him. And if he was murdered, then it will be because someone was getting his own back for some cruel hurt Hugh had done him.'

Alvarez stared at the typed pages. Words. By their very nature limited and enclosed. How could the Superior Chief believe that a report drawn up by a man in another land could ever truly answer the questions? One needed to face the person one was questioning so that one could note where she looked and each changing expression, and hear the tone of her voice, to begin to be able to judge whether she was telling all, some, or none of the truth.

Clearly, Robson had been the complete rotter whether in great or small things; marrying for money, stealing that money and then deserting wife and child; marrying again for social gratification and betraying his wife; sacking a man unnecessarily for a 'crime' far less serious than he had committed; swindling a partner; cheating in a friendly game of golf; discarding women as if they were throwaway objects; pursuing a young and innocent Honor ... But what he—Alvarez—could not be certain, because he had not spoken to Mrs Robson, was whether behind her cool, measured personality, there lurked a spark that could be turned into a raging flame if her sense of loyalty were betrayed ...

'Institute of Forensic Anatomy here. We've concluded the post-mortem of Señor Robson. The cause of death was an alkaloid poison, probably heroin though this has to be confirmed by the laboratory which has samples for testing.'

Which, no doubt, would take many more days to be completed. 'I suppose there's no indication of how the poison was administered?' Alvarez asked.

'None other than that it was taken orally. I'll send a written report to the Superior Chief as well as to you in the hopes that that'll stop him wasting our time by phoning ten times a day.'

After the call was over, Alvarez removed his feet from off the desk and let his chair fall forward on to all four legs. The call merely confirmed the premise on which he'd been working. So nothing had changed, nothing had been gained. He consulted a list of official telephone numbers, dialled the forensic laboratory.

'Hell, no, we haven't had a chance to start the tests yet,' said the assistant, his voice expressing his surprise.

'Then tell me what you can about heroin. For starters, what's the lethal dose?'

'That largely depends on the individual. If he's been addicted for some considerable time, his body can probably tolerate a dose that would knock you or me straight into a wooden casket.'

'What if it's the first time a man's touched the stuff?'

'The lethal dose for a complete amateur is usually put at between point nought six and point one of a gramme.'

'A tenth of a gramme? Not enough to do much more than cover the head of a pin? Are you sure?'

There was a dry chuckle. 'I've no intention of testing the proposition to make certain. Are you forgetting that I'm talking about pure heroin, not the stuff on the streets? That's heavily adulterated, usually with milk sugar though occasionally with something more lethal. The average street fix is four per cent pure so a lethal one would be two grammes, or more.'

After replacing the receiver, Alvarez stared out through the unshuttered window at the sun-covered wall of the building on the opposite side of the road. A tenth of a gramme. A mere dusting of white powder, yet a dusting with the power of death. He shivered. Even the stoutest man's hold on life was so frail it could be fractured by a white shadow. It was difficult to face such truth with equanimity. He reached down to the bottom right-hand drawer of the desk and pulled it open, brought out a bottle of brandy and a glass.

He skimmed through a couple of memoranda from Palma, decided they could be ignored and threw them at the waste-paper basket. He yawned, looked at the desk and was surprised to discover that despite all his efforts, the muddle appeared to be as great as ever. As it was approaching supper-time, the muddle would have to continue.

He had reached the door when the telephone rang. He walked out and shut the door behind himself. Only death could not wait. Downstairs, he bade the duty cabo, who was on the phone, a cheerful good night and carried on towards the outside door.

'Hey! Enrique.'

He came to a stop. 'What?'

'The call's for you. I tried your room, but there was no answer.'

'Try again.'

'But it sounds important.'

'Provided the caller's not the Superior Chief, it isn't.'

'It's someone called Escanellas.'

'Never heard of him.'

'So, tell him you need an introduction before you'll chat.' He held out the receiver.

Very reluctantly, Alvarez retraced his steps and took the receiver, put it to his ear. 'Yes?'

'I've just found a car with a body inside—leastwise, what remains. Gawd, I feel rotten!'

So did he. A moment ago, supper had been imminent; now it was but a distant possibility.

CHAPTER 14

In the quickening of the evening, the mountains between Llueso and Laraix could be either ruggedly beautiful or threateningly dramatic, depending on the quality of the light. Tonight, there was not a cloud in the sky, the light was soft, and they were beautiful. So why did there have to be this ugliness within their shadows? Alvarez looked away from the car and the two men whose unenviable job it was to pack the remains of the driver into a body-bag.

It was obvious what had happened. The car had been going along the rough dirt track—though heavens know why!—and since the driver was almost certainly a foreigner, he'd gone too quickly, the car had skidded on the loose surface, toppled over the edge, and rolled down the steep, rock littered slope until it crashed violently into a pine tree, snapping that off near the base. Because the track was seldom used and because the car had, by the time it was at rest, been all but hidden, it had not been seen until now. (Escanellas had probably been illegally hunting; no Mallorquin bothered about such bureaucratic nonsenses as closed seasons.)

He puffed his way up the slope to the track, mopped his face with a handkerchief. The car had been hired in Palma. So the first thing to be done—in the morning—was to get on to the hirers to identify the driver since he'd not been carrying any papers.

Despite his breathlessness, he lit a cigarette as the two men struggled up the slope with the body-bag and put it in the plain van parked there. They shouted a goodbye and drove off. He crossed to his car, settled behind the wheel, and started the engine. The first drink was going to taste extra good.

The owner of Garaje Cala Grande said over the phone: 'Sounds like ours, since we had one go missing around the beginning of the month, but I'll have to check to make certain.'

Alvarez waited.

'It's ours all right. Hired for two days on the twenty-eighth of last month.'

'Did you report it missing?'

'After the usual three days' grace. We don't do it right away because we're always getting people who don't return the car on the right day and don't bother to tell us they want it for longer.'

'What was the hirer's name and nationality and what address did he give?'

'I've made a note . . . Robert Mills. He'd a British pass-port. Said he wasn't certain where he'd be staying on the island so gave an address in France. Sixteen, Rue de Dun-kerque, La Malon Haute, Basses-Alpes.'

'Did you get any impression of whether he was only on the island for two days or if that was just the time he wanted a car?'

'If I did, I don't remember.'

'That's all for the moment, then. If I need any more information, I'll get back on to you.'

'Hang on a minute . . . You say he was driving along this dirt-track in the middle of nowhere and swerved off to fall down the mountainside?'

'That's right.'

'What was he doing in a place like that?'

'Right now, I've no suggestions.'

'Where does the track lead?'

'To nowhere, really. There was a finca at the end, but

that was abandoned years ago. The land's terraced, but the olives and almonds haven't been pruned since the last person lived in the house. Maybe I'd best send you a map so you know where to find the wreck.'

'When you've the time.'

'There's no hurry? Sounds like you told the insurers it was a brand new car so you don't want them around to discover it was really four years old!'

'Maybe you do things like that your way, but we don't here.'

Alvarez rang off. Why did the name La Malon Haute seem familiar? He'd never been there; hadn't ever visited the Basses-Alpes department . . . He shrugged his shoulders. Like the absence of any personal papers on the dead man and an apparent lack of any inquiries from abroad concerning his disappearance, a point of no real importance.

Salas rang on Thursday morning. 'Where the devil's that report?'

Sweet Mary, he'd forgotten all about it! 'Señor, I posted it days ago,' Alvarez replied.

'Really? I wonder if you can explain why it is that you should be the only inspector in my command whose reports invariably disappear in the post?'

'Perhaps, Señor, the people in the post office here are even more careless than elsewhere.'

'You will have a copy of the report on your files. Fax that to me.'

'I don't have a fax.'

'Is it beyond your wit to find an office or shop that does possess one and which will, for a small fee, transmit the copy to me? See that it's on my desk within the next hour. And perhaps I should add that I shall not listen with a friendly ear to any suggestion that all the telephone lines between Llueso and Palma have collapsed . . . Have you established all the circumstances of Señor Robson's death?'

'I am still waiting to hear from the Laboratory of Forensic Sciences.'

'Waiting being the one occupation at which you excel. Have you anything else to report?'

'No, Señor.'

'Remember. Within the hour!' He cut the connection.

Alvarez scratched his head. Perhaps it was possible to concoct a report inside an hour and fax it to the Superior Chief, but he was damned if he knew how . . . The phone rang again. Salas now demanding the report in half an hour's time?

'It's Roberto.'

'Roberto who?'

'Roberto Parra, you dozy bastard. Are you ready for a surprise? That victim of the car crash up in the mountains died from a shot in the back of the head.'

CHAPTER 15

It had suddenly become very important to know why the name of La Malon Haute was familiar yet, as so often seemed to happen, when most needed his memory seemed to have gone into cold storage. Why should the name of a town or village which he'd never visited, set in a department whose boundaries he'd never crossed, strike a chord? Had he read the name recently? Had it been mentioned on television? . . .

He looked at his watch and was shocked to discover that it was already three-quarters of an hour since Salas had rung. Knowing a little about the way that tortuous Madrileño mind worked, it was a palm tree to a pine kernel that he was watching the time, ready to order his plum-voiced secretary to ring if the fax was not on his desk as the second hand indicated that the hour was up.

Perhaps it was the threat that prompted Alvarez's mind. La Malon Haute was the name of the village in which an English woman had died under suspicious circumstances and the French, ever optimistic, had asked the Mallorquin police to try to trace a white Escort even though they could not give the registration number. What was the date of that request? He searched for, and eventually found amongst the chaos on his desk, the log book in which he was required daily to enter every work item of importance. He was unsurprised to discover that he had failed to record the date of the request; indeed, even the fact that the request had been received. Once again, he tried to force his memory back in time. What that was memorable had happened at about then? Had it been when Dolores had been in a cheerful mood for several days on end? Or around the time of the foguerones when tableaux had been built in the street and, after judging, had been set alight despite the high wind which had added considerably to the danger to all the surrounding houses? Or the day when, to the accompaniment of bangers, a pine tree had been brought down from the Festna Valley to be set up in the village and someone who'd drunk an unusual quantity of wine had greased the trunk so thoroughly that no one had been able to climb to the top to secure the cockerel tied there . . .

He phoned international inquiries and asked them for the number of the police headquarters in La Malon Haute. After a while, he was told that there was no police station there and the nearest one seemed to be in La Malon Basse. He dialled that number and spoke, in French, to a member of the Gendarmerie Brigade. To his surprise, the other knew immediately what he was talking about, a display of efficiency he found slightly disquieting. The request for information concerning the white Escort had been made on the sixth of the month.

'And it was made in connection with the death of an Englishwoman?'

'Mademoiselle Orr—though a forged passport proves that this was not her real name—was found, dead, lying on the rock below the patio of the house she was renting; that was on Monday, the third.'

'Was she murdered?'

'It has been impossible to prove whether the death was accidental or deliberate, though what evidence is available suggested murder. Can you now take us a bit further—was the crashed car the Ford Escort we were looking for?'

'No, it was a hired Seat. The facts this end are that ten days ago an Englishman, Señor Robson, died from heroin poisoning . . .' Concisely, Alvarez detailed the course of the investigation. 'Then this Tuesday, a wrecked car was found up in the mountains and inside was the body of a man who'd been dead some time. He'd no papers on him, but I did not immediately place much significance in this fact because foreigners, and in particular the English, seem unable to understand their importance. However, since it was necessary to identify him, I spoke to the company from which the car was hired and they named him as Robert Mills and said that he'd given as his address—sixteen, Rue de Dunkerque, La Malon Haute. Subsequently it was discovered that he'd been shot before the car had crashed. It seemed rather too much of a coincidence that he should have been living in a village from which we had received a request for information following the death of an Englishwoman.'

'Monsieur Robert Mills is the name of the man who had been staying with Mademoiselle Orr. Whilst not proof, of course, his murder must suggest that it is now beyond question that the mademoiselle also was murdered.'

'If that is so, was Señor Mills the prime suspect?'

'The known facts suggested not. He left the village on the Monday before the mademoiselle's death and was not seen thereafter. The man in the white Escort was seen by an old girl who was positive he was not Mills . . . Can you send us a photograph of Monsieur Robson so that we can check whether he was the driver of the Escort?'

'I think I know where to get hold of a recent one, yes, which is better than a death one. And in return, will you send me a photo of Señorita Orr?'

'Of course. But I'd be interested to know in what connection you need it?'

'Señor Robson kept a videotape in a strong-box in the local bank and when I played this, I discovered it was of a pornographic nature. I'm wondering if she was the woman concerned.'

'Blackmail?'

'It's looking very much like it.'

'I must admit it would be amusing to be able to present the Sûreté with the solution to the problem they've been quite unable to solve!'

After the call, Alvarez considered the facts as he now knew, or could reasonably assume, them to be. It had been Mills, who had called at Robson's house at the end of the previous month . . .

He dialled Salas's number and asked the plum-voiced secretary to put him through to the superior chief.

'Señor, I have just been on the telephone . . .'

'Where is the fax?'

'I am explaining. I have been trying to ascertain whether there is a direct connection between the murder of Señor Mills on this island and the suspicious death, probably murder, of Señorita Orr in La Malon Haute.'

There was a silence, then Salas said: 'Until this moment, I was unaware that a Señor Mills had been murdered here and a Señorita Orr presumably in France. No doubt you considered the facts too trivial to bother me with them?'

'Until the morgue rang me earlier, I presumed Señor Mills's death to be an accident.'

'Might we experiment and start at the beginning? Who is Señor Mills?'

Alvarez explained at some length. 'So you see, Señor, until I learned he had been shot, there was no reason to suspect that his death was anything but an accident.'

'Despite the fact that he was a tourist and therefore most unlikely to explore the byways and the track he'd driven down must clearly have led nowhere; and that he had no papers on him, or even any money?'

'But foreigners do such unpredictable things.'

'I suggest that that is not their prerogative . . . Was it Mills who called at Señor Robson's house at the beginning of the month?'

'I am going to ask the maid if she can identify him.'

'Was Señor Robson the man who was seen in the white Escort in La Malon Haute?'

'I intend to send the French police a photograph of him since they have a witness who should be able to answer that question.'

'Have you questioned the señor's maid to find out if he was away at the relevant time?'

'Not yet. You see . . .'

'It would expedite the investigation if you could show a little initiative and not always wait to be told what to do.'

'Señor, I would have spoken to her before this call had I not wished to keep you fully informed and up-to-date.'

'As you have done concerning the deaths of Señor Mills and Señorita Orr?'

'But I . . .'

'It would undoubtedly pay you to try to remember that

to attempt to excuse the inexcusable is the mark of a fool.'
He rang off.

Alvarez replaced the receiver. A shepherd might scorn a
runty lamb, but he had to bury a dead one. Because he had
enjoyed his unjust sarcasm, Salas had forgotten to return to
the subject of the missing report which should have been
faxed to him.

Luisa stood in the front room of her house. 'He went away
for a day or two, but I couldn't say exactly when that was.'

'Try to fix the date by something else that happened,'
Alvarez suggested.

'Such as what?'

'Well, anything out of the ordinary.'

'I don't know what you're getting at.' Normally, her life
was totally predictable.

'Maybe you bought yourself a new frock?'

'With a family to keep and feed, d'you think I haven't
better things to do with my money?'

Remembering her son, he decided that money spent on
a frock would be far less of a waste. 'Then did anyone call
to have a word with the señor and was surprised to find
him not there?'

She thought, her heavy brow creased. 'Now you mention
it . . . I remember the señorita came along one morning and
was surprised. Only I don't know when that was, either, so
it don't help.'

'If the señorita can place the date, it will. I've one more
question before we leave. Did the señor have any sort of a
gun?'

'He'd a small revolver.'

'There was no sign of that when I searched through his
house after the break-in.'

She shrugged her shoulders.

They drove in his car to the morgue. He left her in the

small, bleakly furnished waiting-room and went through to make certain all was ready. When he returned, her face was expressionless, displaying neither apprehension nor fear at the task which lay ahead. But her attitude, he knew, was stoic, not indifferent—those born into peasant families soon learned that where there was life, there was death. He led the way into a room whose walls as well as floor were tiled and which contained a refrigerated storage cabinet with six drawers. At his signal, the white-coated assistant pulled open the middle right-hand drawer, lifted up the covering sheet so that the head of the dead man was visible.

She nodded. 'That's him what came to the house at the end of last month.'

At last, Alvarez thought, the facts were beginning to meld together.

'You don't usually work in the evening,' Dolores observed.

Alvarez helped himself to an orange from the earthenware bowl in the centre of the dining-room table. 'I don't usually have the Superior Chief sitting on my shoulders.'

'He said you had to go out and work after supper?'

'In effect.'

'To do what?'

'I'd tell you if I could, but it's very confidential.'

'You shaved before the meal!'

Was there nothing she missed? 'I found I'd forgotten to do it this morning.'

'And when has that ever before made you shave in the evening? Do you think me so stupid I'll believe every ridiculous lie you tell me?'

Jaime, his expression bewildered, looked at his wife as he tried to work out what had angered her this time.

'You are going to see her.' It was a statement of fact, not a question.

'Only because the Superior Chief has ordered me to.'

'And did he also order you to shave first?' Her voice rose. 'Has any woman ever suffered as much as me? A cousin who, together with my husband, watches dirty videos and rushes to allow a chit of a foreign girl to make a fool of him when there are decent Mallorquin women with property and husbands under the sod for long enough. Ayee, but the Good Lord took not only Adam's rib, but his brains as well!'

Alvarez peeled the orange, split off a segment, ate. When the Good Lord had decided to make woman, he had acted without forethought.

Some twenty-five minutes later, he left the house—to a resounding sigh from Dolores—and drove down to the port. Honor opened the front door with a welcoming smile that would have produced an even louder sigh from Dolores. 'I was becoming bored with my own company so you arrive to cheer me up! Your timing is impeccable. Come on in and have a drink and only then admit that you've come to ask more questions, not because you seek my company.'

'Why should I lie to you?'

She laughed. 'Shall I let you into a little secret? I think you . . . On second thoughts, that is going to remain my little secret.'

He was certain that had she completed the sentence, he would have been both flattered and embarrassed. Unlike so many of her contemporaries, she did not confuse maturity with senility . . .

He followed her into the sitting-room and sat. She did not ask him what he wanted to drink, but poured out a brandy to which she added three ice cubes. It was as if they'd built up an intimacy between them . . .

'Despite all your gallantry, you have come to ask me more questions, haven't you?' she asked, as she stared at him across the top of her glass of chilled apple juice.

Her words had, thankfully, interrupted thoughts which

were dangerous. 'I'm afraid so. And also to ask you to do something which you may not wish to, even if you can.'

'You're being rather mysterious.'

'Perhaps because I am afraid of hurting you.'

'You won't hurt me when I know you'll do everything you can not to. And anyway, if it's because of Hugh, I've tried to explain how I feel about him. So let's get the work over and done with. What is it you want me to do?'

'Do you have a photograph of Señor Robson?'

'Not of him on his own, only of the two of us together on the beach.'

'Will you lend it to me?'

'Why d'you want it?'

'I need to make a copy so that that can be sent to France.'

'Oh! . . . I don't really know. It was taken only a few days before he . . .'

'Before he died? So that it has become very personal? And for me, or anyone else, to see it would feel like an intrusion into your privacy?'

She looked at him, then away. 'There aren't many who'd understand. You're beginning to worry me, Enrique, because maybe you're seeing so much of me that soon there won't be any secrets left.'

She would always keep her last secret. 'I will arrange it so that in the copy both you and the background are blanked out. Perhaps then most of the privacy will remain?'

'You haven't said why you want to send it to France?'

'There is a possibility that it was he who drove to a village called La Malon Haute.'

'And if he did?'

He side-stepped the question. 'Do you remember one time fairly recently when you arrived at the señor's house and were very surprised because Luisa told you he had gone away?'

'Yes, I do.'

'When exactly was that?'

She stared through the window so that she was in profile. 'The beginning of the month. It was the Saturday and we were supposed to be having lunch and then later on driving into Palma to spend the evening at the Casino. But when I arrived, Luisa told me he'd suddenly left for France.'

'Did he talk about the trip when he got back?'

'Only very vaguely. There'd been a fuss at Barcelona when he'd hired a car and mentioned he was driving into France. They swore he couldn't do that because the car wasn't insured in any other country, he said it almost certainly was for anywhere in the EEC. In the end, he rang the international headquarters who confirmed he was right.'

'Did he mention whereabouts in France he drove to?'

'No. For someone who was usually very open, there were times when he could be secretive. I assumed it had been some sort of business trip. I always imagined he'd continued to dabble in property.'

'Yes, he did.'

'Why are you so interested in this trip? Is it to do with property in France?'

'I'd rather not say for the moment because nothing's yet certain.'

'Is that the real reason? You're not trying to hide something from me for as long as you can because you're afraid it'll upset me?' She studied him. 'Please, Enrique, I'd rather know now than go on guessing, dreaming up ever worse possibilities.'

He decided to tell her. Later he suspected—with a sense of shocked self-contempt—that he'd not really been as reluctant as he'd tried to make out since the truth must blacken Robson in her eyes. 'It all goes back some time. What he told you about his second wife was a lie, and she's someone who values loyalty as much as love. It was he who betrayed the marriage.'

She stared into space. 'How old-fashioned, how much more elegant, to say "betrayed the marriage".'

Was that genuine approval or concealed mockery? 'And he married his first wife because she had money. When he'd stolen all she had, he deserted her, leaving her penniless and with a child. Because she suffered so much, she became an alcoholic and a drug addict.'

'I wonder if that's right?' She cupped her chin in the palms of her hands. 'People are always so glib when it comes to ascribing consequences. I suppose I flatter myself, but I like to think that if I'd been deserted by a husband who'd stolen everything, I'd find the courage to fight back and not turn to an escape route that surely must condemn my daughter to a life of hell.'

He was struck by the way in which her chin, in profile, suggested a tougher, stronger character than normally she appeared to possess. 'I'm certain you would fight all the way,' he said impulsively.

She turned to look full face at him. 'You're certain because you also are a fighter. I can see in your face that you've had to be.'

Her words spun him back in time to Juana-María's lying-in-state. Her coffin had been set out in her small bedroom and throughout the afternoon, relatives and friends had climbed the stairs to stand by it and pray. He had been unable to pray then, or since. The priest had said that it was God's will. But God was supposed to be a loving God . . .

'I'm terribly sorry. I didn't mean to say something that would hurt you.'

'It was many years ago.'

'But time hasn't healed?'

'It's blurred. Perhaps that is as much as one can hope

for.' Was she calling on time to blur her memories of Robson? He was surprised that he still could not decide whether she had been in love with Robson or, as she claimed, had merely liked him.

CHAPTER 16

The first of June was cloudless and by nine-thirty in the morning the temperature was already twenty-nine degrees. In the fields, the sheep, goats, cows, pigs, chickens, ducks, and occasional guinea fowl, with the wisdom of animals, sought shade; on the beaches, with the stupidity of humans, the tourists lay in the full sun.

Alvarez, sweating heavily from the exertion, climbed the stairs, entered his office, and slumped down in the chair behind the desk. After a while, he found the energy to look through the day's post which had been dumped down on top of an irregular pile of files. There was a letter from France. This contained a photograph and a brief note. In the photo, Bridget Orr stood in a field with blue sky as her backdrop. She wore little or no make-up, a breeze had lightly fretted her hair to add a further note of informality, her smile was unforced, her casual clothes, while not hiding her figure, would not have brought a frown to a maiden aunt's forehead. The first day of Spring could not be more wholesome than she.

His disappointment was sharp because he'd been so certain that Bridget Orr was the woman in the video. Where could he have gone wrong? In assuming that Robson had driven to La Malon Haute? After all, the only certainty was that on his return he'd said he'd hired a car in Barcelona which he'd subsequently driven into France. Perhaps it was pure coincidence that this was when Bridget had been murdered. And yet instinct told him there was no coincidence here . . .

He phoned Jospin in La Malon Basse and asked if the photograph of Robson had arrived? It had, but only that morning and Jospin had not yet had a chance to show it to Madame Mallet. Was it very important to know if the old girl identified Robson? Then he'd drop the work he was doing and drive over to La Malon Haute and show her the photo.

He phoned back three-quarters of an hour later. Madame Mallet definitely identified Monsieur Robson as the man in the white Escort.

After replacing the receiver, Alvarez rubbed his forehead in a gesture of tired bewilderment. Since Robson had been driving the Escort, he surely must be concerned in Bridget's death? Yet what motive could he have if it were not connected with that video? . . . He again studied the photograph of Bridget and suddenly recalled the first rule of detection. Make certain you see what is actually in front of your eyes and not what you think, or expect, to be. Bridget in the photo looked so innocent that it seemed sacrilegious to suggest that the dross of life had even come near her and in consequence he had dismissed as ridiculous the possibility that she could be the woman in the video who knew everything there was to know about the dross. But now he ignored the general impression and concentrated on specifics as he had been trained to do. He noted the shape of her head, ears, nose, and chin; the colour and nature of her hair; the degree of arching of her eyebrows; the form and thickness of her lips; the curve of her neck; the set of her shoulders. And they all matched those of the woman in the video . . . As he continued to stare at the photograph, he became convinced that it was her air of virginal innocence even more than her beauty which had lured men on to the hook of blackmail . . .

*

'I am ringing, Señor,' Alvarez said, 'to inform you that the woman in the video which Señor Robson deposited at the bank has been identified as Señorita Bridget Orr. As you will remember, she died under suspicious circumstances at the beginning of the month in La Malon Haute.'

'How positive is the identification?' Salas asked.

'I have no doubts.'

'That hardly answers my question.'

'Señor, I have made a careful and detailed comparison of the physical features of the woman in the photograph and the woman in the video. But should you wish to confirm my judgement, I'll arrange for you to see the video.'

'I have no desire whatsoever to conduct so obnoxious a comparison.'

Yet, typically, was ready to challenge it. 'In addition, it has now been established from a photograph I sent to France that Señor Robson was in La Malon Haute earlier on the day that the señorita died. It would therefore seem reasonable to assume certain facts; that the señor was blackmailing the man who appears in the video; that Señor Mills, who had been living with the señorita, left France to come to this island to speak to Señor Robson, a meeting which resulted in his being shot; that having murdered him, Señor Robson flew to Barcelona where he hired a car and drove to France to murder the señorita; and finally, that several days after his return, he was murdered.'

'By whom?'

'I do not know.'

'From what motive?'

'That is not yet clear.'

'Why should he have murdered both Mills and Señorita Orr?'

'Probably something had gone wrong with the blackmail plan.'

'You told me Robson was a very wealthy man. Why should he engage in blackmail?'

'I've asked myself that question more than once.'

'And no doubt received as many answers?'

'I fear I have received no answer at all.'

'It is clear I need to remind you that at an earlier stage in this case I pointed out that the simplest solution to the murder of the señor would probably be the correct one. Did you not tell me that his gardener bore him a grudge?'

'Yes, Señor.'

'And that he was about to change his will in which he left all his money to his second wife? Are those not two very straightforward motives for murder?'

'But the report from England makes it clear that Señora Robson is wealthy in her own right. So why should she kill him in order to prevent herself being cut out of his will?'

'Are you really so poor a judge of women? Their essential character leads them never to be content with what they have and always to lust for more. That Señora Robson is already wealthy merely means she is even more desirous of becoming still richer. Have you checked whether she has an alibi for the time of Robson's death, by which I mean, the time when the poison was administered?'

'No, Señor.'

'Have you questioned the gardener to see if he has an alibi?'

'No, Señor. You see . . .'

'I see that you have ignored the obvious in order to indulge your malicious enjoyment of the complicated.'

'But how could either Señora Robson or the gardener be connected with the video?'

'Do you find it necessary to harp on pornographic matters because of some unslaked perverted desire?'

'Señor, I am certain that that tape is the key to the murders. Which is why . . .' He stopped.

'Well?'

'Why I am certain I should speak to the French police to find out if they have, in the course of their investigations into the murder of Señorita Orr, discovered anything which must have seemed to them to be quite unimportant, but which in the light of what we now know, may prove to be of vital importance to us.'

'Are you suggesting that you holiday in France?'

'Not holidaying, Señor; eliminating the wilder possibilities so that I can concentrate on the investigation on the lines you have suggested.'

The line went dead.

Was that a rejection or a silent admission that he might as well make the trip, if only to lay to final rest his ridiculous, complicated theories?

He decided it was the latter, on the grounds that Salas would not have hesitated to put into strong words his rejection.

Jospin was considerably younger than Alvarez, but a friendly atmosphere was established from the moment he suggested that rather than sit in his dark and dreary office to talk things over, they adjourn to the café on the other side of the road where they could enjoy a digestif.

They sat at a table set out on the pavement, almost level with a small statue commemorating the fallen in the two World Wars.

'You've no idea why Monsieur Mills was shot?' Jospin asked.

'At the moment, all I can say is that I'm certain the motive has to be connected with the videotape. But in exactly what way, I just do not know.'

Jospin drank. 'I can't help you with that one. And probably not with anything else either, unfortunately.'

'What I'm really hoping is that there is some small fact

which must naturally seem to you to be quite unimportant, yet for me it may have relevance. And something tells me that all it needs to open up this case in one such small fact.'

He drained his glass, signalled to a waiter at another table who nodded, then hurried into the café. 'We'd hoped, of course, especially after news of the murder of Monsieur Mills, that England would provide us with information that would help us solve the murder of Mademoiselle Orr—incidentally, we still do not know her true identity. We ought to have remembered that the bloody English never help anyone but themselves!'

'They've given you no cooperation?'

'When we discovered Monsieur Mills worked for a firm of private detectives in London, we got in touch with them and asked if it had been a case which had brought him to La Malon Haute. After all, that would have explained why his first meeting with the mademoiselle was all frost . . . By the way, are you quite certain that she was the woman in the porno video?'

'Yes.'

'Well, I'm damned if I'd have believed it possible without your guarantee! That photo we sent you made her look the pure, fresh girl one dreamt about when one was young and romantic. It's a difficult world for us men!'

'I feel certain that her greatest asset was that air of complete innocence.'

The waiter came up to the table and put down two glasses, removed the dirty ones. As Jospin added water to his drink, to form rolling clouds in the glass, Alvarez brought a pack of cigarettes from his pocket and offered it.

'Not for me, thanks. I gave it up when my girl became a health freak. The sacrifices we make for love!'

Alvarez lit a cigarette. 'Did the British firm tell you if Mills was here on a case?'

'They regretted they could give us no information because of client confidentiality.'

'How would answering your question breach any confidence?'

'You tell me.'

He drank, enjoying the different flavour of the French brandy.

'I did suggest I wouldn't be able to help!'

'How can one build a house without stones?'

'So how about accepting that we've gone about as far as we can go?' suggested Jospin, only half joking. 'We decide Robson murdered Mademoiselle Orr. You decide Robson murdered Mills.'

'That leaves the murder of Robson to be explained.'

'Go for tidiness and call it an accidental overdose of heroin.'

'Who's accidentally going to overdose himself with two grammes?'

'You didn't say it was enough to get an elephant high! He must really have developed a liking for the stuff.'

'This was probably the first time he'd ever touched it. Which is why it surely cannot have been taken accidentally. So he must have been murdered. But if I am right and that video is the motive for all three murders, then since Señorita Orr and Señor Mills were dead, who was left with reason to kill him? And why should a man so rich as he concern himself with blackmail? I tell you, this is a case filled with irritations.' Alvarez drank. 'When I have a case which refuses to open up, I look for something that doesn't fit the general pattern. Do you know what I mean?'

'Exactly.'

'Here, in France, there is something that doesn't seem to fit. Or am I being stupid and there is a very simple explanation?'

'Pose the problem and I'll see if I can provide the solution.'

'If Señor Mills was on holiday, why should his employers not say so since that would be to break no confidences? Why would a tourist come here since, as attractive as the countryside is, it offers few of the things the average tourist seeks? To see a friend—Señorita Orr? But the evidence is that they most certainly were not friends to begin with. Yet if he was on a case, which surely must be connected with the tape and hence blackmail, why would the señorita, so intimately concerned with the blackmail, welcome into her bed a man whom she must have regarded as a dangerous enemy?'

'I can at least answer that question. The reason was old-fashioned love at first sight.' He chuckled as he saw Alvarez's expression. 'It still does happen! The maid says it was just like something on the telly. At their first meeting, she didn't want to know him, two days later they were laughing together, two more and the beds in her bedroom had been joined together. Love at second sight, maybe I should have said.'

'Why did that happen here?'

'If it'll amuse you, I'll give you the maid's explanation. Love's as much about filling other people's needs as one's own. She actually said that! Ten to one, it comes from *Reader's Digest*. Anyway, there'd always been something odd about the mademoiselle. She was friendly to the locals and ready for a chat, but had no friends who visited her and whom she visited, in spite of the fact that there were several other foreigners in the village who'd have been company. So she was a lonely, unhappy person. It was almost as if she deliberately kept herself to herself . . . Then one day Mills turns up. Although initially she's very far from happy to meet him, she hasn't missed the fact that he takes one look at her and is ready to lie down and have her tramp all over him if that's her scene. So he's eager to offer her what she lacks and she decides to give him what he most wants. And that, according to the good Madame Benflis, is love.'

There was, Alvarez decided, a greater possibility of truth in the maid's suggestion that Jospin, with the cynicism of youth, believed. So what if Mills's love for Bridget had been so overwhelming that not even her admission about her past had affected it? Moreover, had actually spurred him on to don his armour, mount his steed, and sally forth, not to tilt at windmills, but to persuade Robson to release the tape so that it could be destroyed and with it, her past?

Robson had been too aware of the ulterior motives that always prompted his own actions, to believe that Mills would, if presented with the tape, merely destroy it. No one could be that stupid. The true explanation had to be that Bridget had double-crossed him and now she and Mills wanted the video so that in future they could enjoy all the fruits of the blackmail. And Mills would never have made the initial, apparently sentimental approach unless he believed that if it became necessary, he could force him—Robson—to hand over the tape under the threat of exposing him as a blackmailer. Yet what proof could there be of his involvement other than the fact that Bridget, the woman in the tape, would swear to that? He'd never been foolish enough to put anything in writing or to approach the blackmail victim in person . . . And then he'd remembered. In trying to cover himself, he'd left himself open to being exposed. His main bank was in Switzerland, a country renowned for its secrecy in banking. So what safer way of making the regular payments to her—which would buy her silence far more effectively than threats could ever have done—than to ensure they remained under that umbrella of secrecy? He had made her open an account with a bank in Geneva. But what initially had been a safety measure now became a very great danger. If she admitted to the blackmail, her accusation that he was the instigator would almost certainly be sufficient to force exposure of his account; no one could miss the significance of the fact that each month a cheque was drawn on his account and paid into hers . . .

Knowing how wealthy he was, their demands would never be satisfied merely by his handing over the tape. They would bleed him white. So his only way of escape was to murder Mills. But when Mills did not return to France, Bridget would guess what had happened and would seek revenge—obtained by exposing him. Then she also had to be murdered . . .

Everything was now explained but Robson's own death. Had his relief at having escaped exposure been so great that in his euphoria he'd been tempted to try his first fix of heroin, without having the least idea what was a safe amount? That seemed an untenable theory. (And wouldn't Delgado have heard about so large a sale to a first-time buyer?) No, Robson had not died from ignorance, he had been murdered. With Bridget and Mills dead, who had had a motive for murdering him? Someone else he was blackmailing? That question reintroduced another. Why, with all his wealth, had he been blackmailing anyone?

'Dammit, every time I think I've found an answer, I realize the question's moved! And until I'm certain whether or not Robson was a blackmailer, they'll keep on moving.' Alvarez drained his glass. 'You mentioned that Mills was employed by a firm of private detectives. They can say whether he was working for them or was on holiday; and if working, whether it was a case of blackmail.'

'And I also told you that we asked for their cooperation and in return received a sanctimonious lecture on professional confidences.'

'But if they realize that it had become a much larger case, surely they must agree to help?'

'Who is clever enough, or twisted enough, to say how the English will react to anything?'

'True enough. Will you give me the name and address of the firm?'

'Of course. It's in my office and I'll go and get it . . .' Jospin looked at his wristwatch. 'How hungry are you?'

Lunch at home was normally not eaten until around two and the time was only just after midday.

'Maison Blanche is only a couple of kilometres down the road. Choose the eighty francs meal and you can have Escargots Provençal. They're something!'

He was hungry.

CHAPTER 17

The auberge, on the outskirts of La Malon Basse, had once been a coaching inn and this explained the large archway and paved courtyard. The rooms were small, beamed, and had unusually wide floorboards, which sloped this way and that. One all but expected to hear the clop of horses' shoes on the cobbles and the shouts of the ostlers.

Alvarez stared out through the crooked, leaded window at a field in which grew rows of apple trees—ironically not the trees of tradition, but little more than thick branches, tied to wires and no more than three metres high. Here, farming had been forced into the last decade of the twentieth century; on the island, one could still find farms which had not changed from the first decade. He wondered if modern French farmers knew the same fierce, hungry love of the land that the Mallorquin, on his old finca, did?

There was no telephone in the room, so he picked up the

paper on which he'd made a note of the number Jospin had given him and went downstairs. There, he spoke to Madame. She manned the reception desk, served in the small dining-room, and probably bullied her husband in the kitchen since he was the chef. He explained that he wanted to make a telephone call to England. She frowned. Such a call, she said in the tones of someone who counted the centimes as carefully as the francs, cost a fortune and so he would have to pay immediately the call was concluded.

It took a little time to be connected to the receptionist at Ponsonby and Braithwaite. He explained who he was and asked to speak to one of the principals. A couple of clicks and a man said: 'Curling speaking. How can I help you?'

'Señor, my name is Inspector Alvarez, of the Cuerpo General de Policia in Llueso, Mallorca. However, I am speaking to you from La Malon Basse, in France, and my reason for phoning is that I am investigating a murder . . .' Rapidly, he outlined the facts, then concluded: 'So you will understand how important it is for me to know whether Señor Mills was on holiday or working; and if working, the nature of the case.

'Presumably, you have spoken to the French police?'

'It is they who kindly gave me the name of your firm.'

'But clearly failed to understand what I wrote in my letter. Our firm, Inspector Alvarez, at all times respects the confidences of our clients.'

'Naturally, I understand that normally that must be so. But when the French police asked for your help, they could not be certain whether they were dealing with an accidental death or a murder. I am investigating one certain and two virtually certain murders. In such changed circumstances, I'm sure you will wish to help me.'

'Your circumstances may have changed, ours have not. And since there can be no point in prolonging this conversation, you will excuse me if I bring it to a conclusion. Goodbye.'

Alvarez replaced the receiver, scratched the back of his neck. One would have expected even a pompously xenophobic Englishman to have offered at least a measure of co-operation. So why had Curling refused to do so?

'Seventy-three francs fifty centimes,' said Madame, as she held out her hand.

He returned to his room, sat on the chair whose legs looked like gruyère thanks to woodworm, and lit a cigarette. To the question he had asked himself a moment ago, one answer was obvious. Mills's firm had been employed by the man who was in the video and was being blackmailed and he was in a position of such importance that the firm had been ordered not to cooperate even with the police.

The more he thought about it, the more certain he was that the whole key to solving the murders lay in persuading someone in Ponsonby and Braithwaite that the truth must be told, under the guarantee that their client's confidence would be observed. Obviously, there was no hope that a second telephone call could achieve this. Only a personal approach would succeed. He had to travel to London and for this he needed Salas's approval. Yet was anything more certain than that this would not be forthcoming? He remembered that the wise farmer did not tell his neighbour the other's ram was in his flock until it had had time to tup them all.

London frightened him, as did any large city, because here one ceased to be an individual. Life had no more meaning than death.

The reception area at Ponsonby and Braithwaite was all discreet gloss, right down to the young, smart receptionist, whose vowels were at home in South Kensington. One of the phones on her large desk sounded and she answered the call. That concluded, she smiled a toothpaste smile and said: 'Mr Curling will see you now. Would you go through that door and into the first room on the right.'

He was certain that had he been of any importance, she would have led the way.

Curling, standing behind the desk, was dressed in a bespoke pin-striped suit. He said, in clipped tones: 'Good morning.'

'Good morning, Señor.' Alvarez expected Curling to observe normal courtesies, come round the desk, shake hands with a smile, and say words to the effect that it was a pleasure to meet his visitor. He did not.

'Please sit.'

He sat. 'Señor, I am here because . . .'

'Correct me if I'm wrong, but you are here because you have chosen to misunderstand what I said to you over the phone and are intending to ask about a case we have handled.'

'Yes, that is so. You see . . .'

'I will tell you once more, very simply, that we respect our clients' confidences absolutely. This means that neither I nor any other member of the firm will answer any question which threatens such confidences.'

'But I am a policeman.'

'A Spanish policeman. However, even were you an English policeman, I would say no differently.'

'It was one of your employees who was murdered.'

'However distressing the facts, they do not alter principles.'

He looked too desiccated to be distressed by anything. 'You don't feel that in these exceptional circumstances, and in order to help the investigations, perhaps certain information could be given without compromising those principles?'

'It is the strength of our country, Inspector Alvarez, that it is our wont to observe rules, not to bend them.'

'I wasn't trying to suggest . . .'

'It appears that I need to be even more explicit. Our founders laid it down that the firm should serve the carriage trade—a concept which has been faithfully followed although one now prefers the term profession rather than trade. Our clients, therefore, are men and women from the highest social levels and such people rightly expect absolute discretion. This we guarantee them.'

Gloomily, Alvarez said: 'At the very least, Señor, surely you can tell me whether Señor Mills visited La Malon Haute because he was on holiday or engaged on a case? Providing the answer cannot possibly compromise your ethical standards.'

'Coming from Spain, as you do, I feel it would be a waste of both our times for me to try to explain why you are incorrect. I can tell you nothing. Good morning.'

Alvarez stood. 'I wonder if before I go you'll satisfy my curiosity on one point, Señor? Was it one of your employees who, contrary to your immaculate standards, broke into Señor Robson's house after his death and turned everything upside down in an effort to find the pornographic tape?'

Curling held his face down so that his expression was not readily visible and tried to make out that he was already deep in work.

Food usually restored Alvarez's good humour, but lunch signally failed to do so. The steak had surely died on the hoof, the chips were soggier than yesterday's political speech, and a thin glass of even thinner wine cost more than a litre of wholesome vino corriente on the island.

Misery bred misery. What was he going to say to the Superior Chief? Had he learned something of importance from Ponsonby and Braithwaite, he could have suggested this was excuse enough for his unauthorized trip, but he had learned nothing.

The waiter asked him what he'd like for sweet and in a moment of rashness, born of his fears, he asked for another glass of wine. The waiter gave him an odd look.

He sipped the wine since to drink it would be to empty the glass in a trice and perhaps it was this unwelcome restraint which prompted his brain. There was another possible source of information in England. Señora Mills. How to obtain her address? If he asked Ponsonby and Braithwaite for it, he would be refused. But to kill a cat, it was not essential to cut its throat. He could telephone them and, posing as a member of the French Embassy, say that there were some personal effects of the dead man to be returned to the widow, might he please have her address? In a firm as refined as they, it was odds on that no one would have the wit to distinguish between a Frenchman's and a Spaniard's speaking English . . . He was so cheered up by this inspired suggestion that he signalled to the waiter and asked for a third glass of wine. The waiter gave him an even odder look.

He telephoned from one of the call boxes in Piccadilly tube station. The receptionist said she'd put him through to Mr Smythe.

'How can I help you?' Smythe asked.

Alvarez explained that the embassy had received a request from the Sûreté Nationale in Sarignon for the address of Madame Mills, widow of Monsieur Robert Mills. They wished to return his few personal belongings to her.

'Hang on and I'll get it.'

He waited.

'The address is thirty-two, Heather Field Lane, Ealing.'

He thanked the other, rang off.

*

The taxi came to a stop. 'There you are, mate,' said the driver.

He climbed out on to the pavement, paid the fare, and added a tip twice as large as he considered reasonable. As the taxi drove away, he studied the house and those on either side. Small, semi-detached, each with a pocket-handkerchief garden. Their paintwork was in good order, their gardens weeded and colourful, yet he found them depressing because they seemed to him to speak of greyness. Was this simply because they never knew sharp Mediterranean sunshine?

He opened the front gate, walked up the short flagstone path, stepped into the tiny porch with an imitation stained-glass side window and rang the bell. The door was opened by a woman who had a square face, a mouth that was surely a stranger to passion, and the squarest of square chins. Middle-age had not been kind to her body, but had she had the taste to dress more circumspectly, this fact would not have been so obvious. 'Señora Mills?'

The moment he betrayed himself to be a foreigner, her manner became both suspicious and hostile. 'What d'you want?'

'My name is Enrique Alvarez and I am an inspector in the Cuerpo General de Policia in Mallorca; in Llueso, to be precise.'

'Well?'

'As you will know, most tragically your husband died on the island. May I say how sorry I am that this should be so.'

She brushed aside his commiserations. 'So what d'you want now?'

'To ask you some questions, if I may?'

She hesitated, then said: 'I suppose you'd better come in.'

He entered a small hall that was in half-light because

there was only one small, circular window above the door. Everything seemed to be coloured brown.

She shut the door. 'Why come here to ask me questions?'

'Because the answers may help me discover who killed your husband.'

'How would I know anything about that? Ask her, not me.'

'You are referring to Señorita Orr?'

'Who else?'

'I fear that she also is dead.'

'When?'

'She died after your husband, but her death was known some time before his was.'

'No one told me.'

She sounded annoyed. The unchristian thought occurred to him that this was because she had been denied the good news until now.

Without a word, she half turned, opened a door, and went through into the room beyond. After a moment's hesitation, he followed her. This room was as brown as the hall. Perhaps brown became a substitute for grey.

A ginger cat had been on one of the armchairs, but when it saw him, it leapt down on the floor and raced behind the television set.

'He doesn't like strangers,' she said, with satisfaction. She began to call, 'Darcy, Darcy,' but the cat remained half hidden. She sat on the chair that the cat had so recently vacated. 'I can't tell you anything because I hadn't seen him for over a month.'

'Did you perhaps have a letter from him?'

'And if I did?'

'It might well have a small piece of information in it that would help me. I will be perfectly frank, Señora, the motive for his death is a mystery and until I can uncover what that was, it may well remain so.'

'You must be soft!' she said with angry, rude contempt. 'It was her.'

'You think the señorita was in some way responsible for his death?'

'He wouldn't be dead if he hadn't gone off with her, would he?'

'That, I fear, is possibly true, but I don't think she bears any direct responsibility. Would you mind very much telling me what he wrote in his letter?'

'He said he wasn't coming back.'

'Did he explain why this was?'

Her tone became hurt and even more bitter. 'He'd discovered what love really meant. He was sorry to desert me, but he couldn't help himself . . . He was always weak.'

'Did he mention how he had come to meet the señorita? Was it through his work?'

She ignored the question. 'Said he felt twenty years younger when he was with her. How could he be such a fool?'

'Did he write about anything other than how he felt?'

'He said he'd soon be sending me money so I didn't have to worry. I wouldn't have to worry, when he'd gone off to live with some rotten little tart!'

'Why do you call her a tart?'

'She's stolen my husband, hasn't she?'

'I just wondered if you'd some particular reason for saying that?'

She didn't bother to answer. 'And me with the mortgage to pay, food to buy, and only the little money my mother left me. I'm going to have to move.'

The house depressed him, but he could appreciate that for her it was a home she dreaded leaving. 'Did you hear from him again?'

'Just that one letter. Telling me how wonderful life was.

When I'd spent twenty years cooking for him, mending his clothes, putting up with that.'

He supposed that 'that' meant sex. If she had found it so distasteful, it was small wonder that her husband had found himself lyrically transported into the realms of the Karma Sutra when he'd met Bridget.

The tears came suddenly.

He said how sorry he was, even while acknowledging that words were virtually useless. He had had to learn that grief was like pain, its subjective boundaries lay entirely within oneself and sympathy seldom eased it for any length of time—indeed, there were occasions when the words even exacerbated it because the speaker was not also suffering.

She stopped crying and wiped the tears from her cheeks. 'I read the letter through twice and then d'you know what I did?'

'No, Señora.'

'I'd given him a pipe for his last birthday; a very special one. He'd not taken it with him so I smashed it to pieces with an axe. And then I went up to the spare bedroom he used as an office when he had to do work at home. I never touched his papers, like I never read his letters unless he wanted me to. But I looked through everything in the room to try and find the tart's address, which wasn't in his letter.'

It clearly had not occurred to her that her husband had not known Bridget before he'd left home and therefore it was unlikely there would be a record of her address. 'Did you find it?'

'No.'

'Did you come across any reference to his trip to France?'

'Only the usual list of expenses he always had to keep.'

'How were those expenses listed?'

'Under a name.'

'Can you remember what that name was?'

'What's it matter?'

'It could be important.'

The cat finally moved from behind the television and stood in front of the fireplace, surveying Alvarez with suspicious dislike.

'He won't hurt you, lovie,' she said. 'Come to mother.'

The cat made no move. She stood, crossed the room to pick it up, returned to her chair. As she stroked it, she said: 'I had to have him seen to because he was such a naughty boy, always after the girls.'

Perhaps she would have liked to have done the same to her husband?

'You're not like him, are you, lovie? You're going to stay with mummy. You'll never go away with some horrible lady.' She leaned forward and kissed the cat's head.

He wondered if she'd become slightly mentally unhinged by her husband's desertion and subsequent death? 'Señora, what was that name?' he asked, his tone sharper than he'd intended because her behaviour disquieted him.

'Sir John Varley,' she answered. Her expression changed and suggested that she was surprised to discover she had remembered.

He waited at crossroads for a taxi, but none appeared so he began to walk in the direction in which he hoped the tube station lay. Sir John Varley. Not unnaturally, he did not recognize the name, but the title told him the other was a British aristocrat—the owner of a vast estate who spent his days hunting, fishing, and shooting and his nights claiming the right of *ius primae noctis*. A man who would not know such women as Bridget Orr even existed. So why should it have been his name on the list?

He stopped and used a handkerchief to mop the sweat from his face. The day was at best warm, but the pavements were iron hard and it was a long, long time since he'd walked half as far. He asked a fellow pedestrian how far it was to the tube station and was told only a mile, as if that were no more than a mere stroll; but a mile was more than a kilometre and a half . . . To try to take his mind off his present misery, he reviewed his meeting with Mrs Mills. And in doing so, he noted something he'd previously missed. In Mills's letter to his wife he'd written that he'd soon be sending her money. Yet how could he have hoped to do so? He'd left everything he possessed in England because he'd been expecting to return. In France, where the air was charged, he'd met Bridget Orr. Love was a mystery; were it not, it would not be love. That mystery had caused him to throw away his past, which meant he was penniless . . .

Bridget had received enough money from Robson to allow her to lead a low-key life. But contrary to the fiction, two people could not live as cheaply as one and so there was no way in which Mills could have been in a position to send a single penny back to his wife unless . . . She had confessed to the source of her money. He had thought that where there was some, there must be more—after all, Robson could always squeeze the extra out of the victim. He had failed to realize something that would have been obvious had love not scrambled his wits—Robson, being a blackmailer, knew full well that only death could guarantee an end to blackmail . . . Alvarez remembered how he had originally decided Mills had approached Robson in order that Bridget's past might be expunged. He was astonished to think how idealistically naïve he had been.

CHAPTER 18

The assistant pointed to the far side of the small room, set apart from the main library area, in which were kept reference books. 'You'll find several volumes over there that might help, such as *Who's Who* and various year books. Do you know which particular field he's in?'

'I'm afraid not, Señorita.'

'Señora,' she said shyly. She briefly showed him her left hand. 'I was married six months ago.'

'Then indeed I congratulate you, Señora.'

'Are you from Spain?'

'Mallorca.'

'That's where we had our honeymoon! . . . Look, let me see if I can help. What is this man's name?'

'Sir John Varley.'

She said, her voice high with surprise: 'And you don't know who he is . . . I'm sorry, of course you wouldn't. I mean, I don't know the name of the people in your government.'

'He is a minister?'

'That's right, only I'm not exactly sure which one. George—my husband—says I ought to pay much more attention to things, but I can't see it really matters very much. I mean, they're all much of a muchness. It's promises before the election and forget it afterwards. Though George does say that Sir John's the only honest one in the present lot, and coming from him, that's really something! . . . Look, you sit down at the table and I'll bring you what books we have that'll tell you about him.'

She put four books down on the table. He opened the first one and found it contained short biographical sketches,

set out in alphabetical order. He flipped through the pages
to the Vs. Sir John Varley's entry was longer than most.
Son of Sir Roger Varley, the fourth baronet and a member
of Parliament for twenty-six years. Sir John Varley's seat
(it took Alvarez some time to work out what they meant)
was Varley Hall, in Shropshire. He had been elected to
Parliament thirteen years before; made his mark as a good
speaker with a deceptively polite manner; appointed a PPS,
an Under Secretary of State, and Minister of State for
the countryside; was generally expected to reach cabinet
rank; acknowledged to be respected almost as much by his
opponents as by those in his own party . . .

He closed the book and did not bother to consult the
other three. Since it was inconceivable that such a man
could have had any direct involvement with the blackmail,
either it was one of his subordinates who had (and his name
had been used by Mills merely as a means of identifying
the case) or Mrs Mills had remembered the wrong name.
There was only one way of finding out which was the correct
answer.

The half-mile long drive was lined with oaks so venerable
that the lower branches of several had had to be supported.
The house was Elizabethan, in the classical E shape, and
one of the finest surviving examples in the country, so in
harmony with the surroundings that it might almost have
grown rather than have been built.

He parked by the side of the raised, circular flowerbed
in the middle of the drive, left the car and crossed the gravel
to the simple porch. The wrought-iron bell-pull was in the
shape of a fox's head. It was like stepping back in time . . .

The heavy, panelled wooden door was opened by a thin
and angular man, dressed in black coat and striped
trousers, who studied him and then said, 'Good morning,'

in a tone which pointed out that the tradesmen's door was
to the rear.

'I should like, please, to speak with Sir John Varley.'

'May I have your name?'

Alvarez gave it. The butler showed no surprise, merely
continuing disapproval. 'Step inside, please.'

Alvarez entered the very large hall to face three suits of
armour, and above them, on the wall, several geometrical
designs made from pistols and swords.

'Wait here.'

The butler crossed the hall, opened a door on the far
side, passed through and out of sight. Alvarez looked
around himself, eager to take in every aspect of a world
that until now he had only seen on film. In addition to the
suits of armour and the arms' displays, there were several
paintings in heavy gilded frames of serious looking men in
varying styles of dress, two seated china dogs by the huge
open fireplace, crossed flags, the material of which had so
deteriorated that it had to be supported by fine wire mesh,
and a heavy, ornately carved oak table on which was a
selection of magazines . . .

The butler reappeared. 'Come this way, please.' He was
as careful to add 'please' as he was to forget 'sir'.

Alvarez followed him down a short, dark, panelled passage and into a room that was contrastingly bright because
it faced south and sunlight came through the two large
windows.

'Inspector Alvarez, my Lady,' said the butler. He
inclined his head, left.

Lady Varley, who was seated, briefly inspected Alvarez.
It was clear that she did not miss the open neck, the well
worn coat, the baggy trousers, or the scuffed shoes. 'I
understand that you are a Spanish policeman?'

'Yes, Señora . . . That is, yes, Lady Varley.' No one, he
thought, could mistake either her nationality or her rank.

Tall, angular, her movements less than fluid, she was
dressed in a twin set whose colours did not suit her complexion; her hairstyle was wrong for her oval face; her eyes
were light blue and frosty, her nose Roman, her mouth
unused to smiling; her shoes were sensible and far from
flattering. The pearls in her necklace, which drew attention
to how scrawny was her neck, were so large that normally
they must have been cultivated, but to assume that she
would have worn anything but natural pearls of the highest
quality would have been perverse.

'Why are you here?'

'I have come to speak with your husband because I think
he may be able to help me.'

'That would seem highly unlikely.'

'Lady Varley . . .'

She interrupted him. 'What precisely leads you to
imagine that there is any way in which my husband can
possibly assist you?'

'I am investigating a murder which took place near
Llueso at the end of April.'

'Is that supposed to be an answer?'

'The thing is . . .'

'It is ridiculous to imagine that your investigation could
be of the slightest concern to him.'

He doggedly continued. 'The murdered man's name was
Mills and I am certain he was murdered by a fellow
Englishman, Hugh Robson. Señor Robson also murdered
Señorita Orr, with whom Mills had been living. Then, in
the middle of last month, he also died, almost certainly
from an overdose of heroin. I believed he was murdered
because he was blackmailing someone.'

'It would seem advisable not to visit the island.'

'It's not really like that. The island is very beautiful . . .'

'Beauty is a matter of opinion.'

'It is true that in the summer perhaps there are many

people on the beaches and that some places, such as Magalluf, are not as attractive as they once were, but inland all is different. In the mountains, there is such beauty that a man is refreshed . . .'

'Are you sure you're a policeman and not the representative of a travel agent?'

'It's just that I should like you to understand what my island is really like.'

'If I wished to know, I would ask. I am a very busy person, so perhaps you will come to the point and explain exactly why you wish to speak to my husband.'

'As I've said . . .'

'Then there'll be no need to repeat yourself.'

'Señor Mills worked for a firm of private investigators and whilst on a case in France, he met Señorita Orr. At the end of April, he travelled from France to Mallorca and it was there that he was murdered. In the course of my investigations I've talked to Señora Mills and she told me that on papers connected with her husband's work, the name of Sir John Varley was written. That is why I am here now to speak to him.'

'I fail utterly to understand why that should follow.'

'I think it probable that someone who works for your husband was being blackmailed by Señor Robson because this person appeared on a video with Señorita Orr in unusual circumstances.'

'What does that mean?'

'Well . . . well, their behaviour was of a pornographic nature.'

'Your island is clearly home to all that is most objectionable about modern life and I have no wish to hear any more about it. So perhaps you'll leave.'

'Lady Varley, I should very much like to speak to your husband . . .'

'I can assure you that the wish will not be reciprocated.'

'But this is very important . . .'

'To someone who spends his days dealing with matters of state, it will seem both unimportant and repellent.'

'Is he here?'

'He is not.'

'Then could you be kind enough to tell him that I should be very grateful if I might have a word with him. I'm staying at the Swan Hotel in Easting Cross.'

She rang for the butler.

He was in the bar of the hotel, dismally counting the change from a five pound note, when one of the employees looked in and called out: 'Inspector Alvarez?'

'That's me.'

'You're wanted on the phone in the foyer.'

He stood and picked up the glass. Thankfully, Sir John Varley was going to be very much more pleasant and cooperative than his wife had been. He left the bar and went into the foyer, where the receptionist motioned in the direction of the call-box by the far wall.

He lifted the receiver. 'This is Inspector Alvarez of the Cuerpo General de Policia . . .'

There was a flood of furious Spanish. 'Do you think I need to be told that?'

He wondered if both ears and mind were playing him tricks? 'Is that you, Señor?'

'Just what the devil are you doing in England?'

'I've been following certain leads . . .'

'You will catch the next available plane back to the island. You will report to me the moment you land. Is that simply enough put for you to understand?'

'Yes, but . . .'

The line was dead.

He replaced the receiver, raised his glass and absent-mindedly drained it. One thing was now all too clear.

Lacking the discovery of any evidence that would justify his unauthorized trip from France to Britain, he was in trouble.

He died several times as the plane came in to land, but the wings stayed stuck on to the fuselage, the engines didn't cut out, and the tyres didn't blow off. As they came to a halt, he opened his eyes and began once more to breathe normally.

There was the usual wait before the buses arrived to drive them to the terminal; and the usual, even longer wait before the carousel began to bring the luggage, but eventually he was able to pick up his suitcase and leave the arrival hall.

Outside the terminal building, he hailed a taxi and told the driver to take him to Llueso.

CHAPTER 19

Dolores hugged him for several seconds before announcing, as she released him, that in honour of his safe return, she had cooked Estofat de xot. Jaime, once she'd returned to the kitchen, crossed to the sideboard and brought out a bottle of brandy and two glasses. Juan and Isabel, having unwrapped their presents, went out to play in the road until lunch was ready.

'So how was it?' Jaime asked, as he poured out two drinks. He did not wait for an answer. 'If you knew what it's been like here! All the time you've been away, she's been worse than usual. When you go away, she worries and that makes her absolute hell! You're not going to believe this, but last night she stopped me having a second coñac after supper. I said, how can a man digest his grub without help . . . There you were, enjoying yourself and I couldn't even have a second coñac!'

'As a matter of fact, things were just as difficult . . .'

'She's always like that when you go away. And if there's a plane crash anywhere in the world, she starts hiding all the bottles, even the wine, and it's a hell of a job to find 'em. But that wouldn't concern you, would it? You're all right.'

One man's trouble was another man's irrelevance. After lunch, Alvarez thought, he was going to have to phone Salas.

After a refreshing siesta followed by coffee and two slices of coca, he rang Palma. The plum-voiced secretary told him to wait. He waited.

'You're at the airport, are you? Then get over here immediately. I expect you in a quarter of an hour.'

'I'm afraid I shall be a little over an hour, Señor.'

'Why?'

'I have to drive from Llueso.'

'What the devil are you doing there? I thought I ordered you to report to me the moment you landed on the island?'

'Indeed, Señor. And that is exactly what I would have done had I not suffered an attack of air sickness which left me almost supine. In those circumstances, I thought it necessary to return home to recover sufficiently to be able to answer any questions you may have.'

'May have? . . . Do you remember what I said when you asked for permission to fly to France?'

'In actual fact, Señor, on that occasion you didn't say anything. You just slammed . . . replaced the receiver.'

There was a silence. 'I have to confess,' Salas finally said, 'that when talking to you, the temptation to do just that is ever present. I said that you might travel to France to confer with the French police, but having done so, you were to return here. Do you remember me saying that?'

'I'm afraid I don't.'

'Your memory, evidently, is highly selective. Which explains how you managed so conclusively to forget the terms under which an officer is permitted to conduct an inquiry in a foreign country.'

'I do realize that I should first have had the permission of the English police, only in the circumstances . . .'

'In the circumstances, you simply could not be bothered to observe any of the rules. Not for you the trouble of drawing up an official request; not for you the bother of forwarding that request in the most unlikely event that I approved it; not for you the courtesy of not setting foot on English soil until your visit had been officially welcomed.'

'Since I was already in France, I thought . . .'

'An exaggeration. No police officer can be credited with thinking who travels to England without authorization, who conducts an investigation there without the knowledge of the English police, and who, no doubt in a moment of inspiration, insults the wife of one of the country's most prominent and respected politicians.'

'Señor, I did no such thing.'

'I have been grossly misinformed? Then you can now tell me the true facts. You did not fly from France to England without my express permission?'

'When I said I did not, I meant . . .'

'Just answer my question.'

'Well, I . . . I suppose that strictly speaking, I did.'

'Once in England, though, any inquiry you conducted was with the full knowledge of the English authorities?'

'All I did was talk to a member of a firm of private investigators and Señor Mills's widow.'

'Without the required official approval? But to a man of your liberal attitudes, a mere technical breach of a rule is no breach . . . Still, at least one can surely be certain that not even you could have visited the home of Sir John Varley and insulted his wife.'

'Of course not, Señor.'

'You did not go anywhere near his house?'

'As a matter of fact, I did visit it, hoping to have a word with him.'

'Did you succeed?'

'Unfortunately, he was away that day.'

'Did you, then, have any word with his wife?'

'Yes, but I was very careful to be polite.'

'So it is ridiculous to suggest that you told her her husband was a murderer?'

'Absolutely ridiculous.'

'Or that he was a drug addict?'

'I said no such thing.'

'And you certainly did not begin to suggest he'd been indulging in obscene behaviour?'

'All I said to Lady Varley was that I'd like to ask her husband if he could explain why his name appeared on a list of expenses which had been drawn up by Señor Mills who had been detailed to investigate Señorita Orr. I may have added that there was reason to believe there had been a blackmailing plot based on a pornographic video and that Señorita Orr was an accomplice to blackmailing Señor Robson, but at no time . . .'

Salas lost his air of measured, ironic calm and began to shout. 'You added blackmail! You accused a noble Englishman of impeccable character not only of murder, drug addiction, sexual deviance, but blackmail as well? In your haste, did you forget rape, arson and treason?'

'Señor, I never suggested that he was in any way directly involved . . .'

'I am a reasonable man. So I will not express myself as another well might. But I am forced to point out that your insane behaviour has forever stained the honour of the Cuerpo General. Lady Varley, obviously with every reason, complained to her husband about your disgusting allegations. Sir Varley—a politician of such stainless reputation that he is hardly a politician at all—complained to the Spanish ambassador. He spoke to the Prime Minister, who spoke to the Minister of the Interior, who spoke to the director-general, who telephoned me and ordered me to investigate the matter . . . You are suspended from duty until an official inquiry is held to decide whether or not you are guilty of conduct prejudicial to the corps and the country. When you are found guilty, you will be discharged with ignomy and infamy. On that day I shall feel that the burden I bear when trying to maintain law and order has been immeasurably lightened.' He cut the connection.

Bewildered, Alvarez replaced the receiver. All right, he should have had Salas's authority before flying to England; it was possible to suggest that when he'd spoken to Curling and Señora Mills, he had been conducting an investigation without the prior knowledge and permission of the British police; but when talking to Lady Varley, he had not suggested her husband was guilty of any crime. But who was going to take his word against hers? Why should she lie? The obvious answer was, she wouldn't. No, she had done no more than make certain that a rumpled, clumsy Mallorquin detective was admonished for his presumption in coming to her mansion and asking to speak to her husband about a matter so obnoxious it could not begin to concern him, and as her complaint had been passed from one great person to another, it had been enlarged, garbled, utterly distorted . . .

He wandered back to the kitchen.

Dolores looked up and saw his expression. 'Santa María, what has happened?'

'I've been suspended.'

'What do you mean?'

'The Superior Chief has been told by the Director-General that I insulted the wife of a very important person in England. But I didn't. I was as polite as I could be.'

'Tell the Superior Chief that.'

'I have. But he never believes me anyway. And so I am to be tried before an internal tribunal and dismissed from the service, without a pension.'

'You must fight!'

He slumped down on the chair by the table. 'To fight successfully, I must prove that the Director-General, the Minister of the Interior, the Prime Minister, the Spanish Ambassador in London, and Lady Varley, are all mistaken. How can any man do that, let alone an inspector in Llueso whose Superior Chief will be only too glad to see him thrown out?'

She did nothing for several seconds, then left the kitchen in a rush. When she returned, she had a bottle of brandy in one hand and a glass in the other.

The phone rang and Dolores left the dining-table. Jaime leaned across to say in a low voice: 'What d'you reckon has got her in such a good mood?' Quick to seize an advantage, he refilled his tumbler with wine.

'She's doing what she can to cheer me up,' Alvarez replied.

'Why should you need that any more than me?'

'I'm in deep trouble.'

Jaime could be extraordinarily crass. 'If that gets her this pleasant, keep it up.'

Dolores returned. 'It's for you, Enrique. The Laboratory of Forensic Sciences.'

He left and went through to the front room.

'I've been trying to get you in your office,' the caller

said, 'but they told me you're not going in there any more. Retired, have you?'

'Not yet.'

'Just resting? Wish I had that sort of a job . . . I'm calling to say we've completed the tests in the Robson case and can confirm that the cause of death was poisoning by heroin. The fatal dose was about point two of a gramme, pure.'

Did he now give a damn what was the cause of Robson's death? Nevertheless, he asked: 'Was it taken pure or in the usual cut form?'

'The evidence—which is very far from certain—suggests pure.'

'I've never heard of that being on the street, so where the hell d'you think his murderer obtained it?'

'Direct from an importer? Or maybe there's someone who's enough of a chemist to know how to separate the heroin from the adulterant—if it's milk sugar that was used, it's not a difficult task, just a laborious one.'

A murderer who spent a small fortune buying on the streets and then separating out the adulterant to produce a fatal dose which weighed only a fifth of a gramme? Why go to such trouble? To administer it without its presence being suspected? But how did one administer so bitter a substance without the victim's becoming aware of the fact? He put that question.

'I was going to come to that. The short answer is, we don't know; the long answer is, we have a suggestion. You remember sending us a whole range of things to see if any of 'em showed traces of poison? None did. But the bottle of hay fever pills has suggested something. Separate the two halves of a capsule, empty it, replace the contents with pure heroin, plug the two halves together and return the capsule to the bottle. Then there's a fatal time bomb. We checked the few remaining capsules in the bottle, but they were clear. So that's an idea, no more.'

Not even a probability. Yet it told Alvarez who had murdered Robson. Timing was everything. Yet sometimes, timing was nothing.

Luisa was using a long-haired paint brush to clean the dust from the downstairs shutters of her house when Alvarez drew up in his car. She watched him step on to the pavement, nodded, said nothing.

'Have you time for a word?' he asked.

'No.'

He smiled. 'The woman who works all day, keeps her husband at bay.'

'That's all you men ever think about!' She put the paint brush down on the sill, by the side of the window-box full of climbing geraniums, led the way down a narrow passage and through to a small, square patio at the back of the house. Two plastic seats were near a tangerine tree, on which the hard fruit was the size of small marbles, and she moved one into the shade before she sat. When he'd done the same, she said: 'What's there to talk about?'

'The señor's hay fever. Did he suffer from it all the time?'

'Not all, but much. And it became real bad when the pine trees were in flower or the pampas-grass was out. I've seen him sneeze until he looked like exploding.'

'Was anything affecting him badly shortly before he died?'

She thought back. 'I can't remember.'

'You didn't notice him taking a pill on the day before he died?'

She shook her head.

'Well, thanks for all your help.'

'D'you know what went on?'

'I do now.'

'It's taken you long enough. Felix says it would take your lot a lifetime to find out who won the war.'

'He could well be right, seeing that a lot of the people who went into hiding up in the mountains in those days are now running around in Mercedes.'

CHAPTER 20

Alvarez parked, walked up the short path, and knocked on the door of the bungalow. After a moment, Honor opened the door.

'Sorry to keep you, Enrique, but I was sunbathing.'

'I'm sorry to have disturbed you.'

'It's just as well you have or I'd have overcooked and suffer all the horrors that people keep talking about. My trouble is, I just adore sunbathing. Why are fun things so often bad for us?'

'Nature doesn't like us to enjoy ourselves for very long.'

'What a thoroughly miserable explanation! You obviously need a stiff drink to cheer you up, so let's rush you one.'

He followed her into the sitting-room and sat. She went across to the sideboard, poured him a brandy. He watched her pour an orange juice for herself and as she moved, her tight-fitting T-shirt outlined her right breast in sharper detail . . .

She went through to the kitchen for ice, returned, handed him a glass, sat, raised her glass. 'Here's to us having lots and lots of fun!' She drank. 'Have you been away?'

'What makes you think I might have been?'

'I haven't seen you for ages.'

There was no room for ambiguity; she'd missed him and

welcomed his return! 'I had to go to France and then on to England.'

'Was it business or pleasure?'

'Had it been pleasure, I would not have gone.'

'That's thoroughly Irish!' She laughed. 'And a blind, to boot! Tell the truth and shame the devil, you're far from the stay-at-home you so often try to make out, aren't you?'

He smiled. 'I hope that's right. But when this island offers everything, who will willingly leave it?'

'That is self-satisfaction unlimited. But if I'm going to be honest, I'll have to admit that if someone silenced all the barking dogs at night and radios in the day, this island is as near to heaven as mortals are allowed to get . . . You implied it was business took you abroad, but I'll bet there was time left over for pleasure?'

'There was very little of that around. The truth is, the trip ended in disaster.'

'Oh Lord, that sounds really grim! Exactly what happened?'

'Let's talk of other things. We have a saying, pleasure should be shared, suffering endured.'

'All very noble, but that doesn't take account of either my curiosity or the chance to help.'

He said quietly: 'Then will you answer a question?'

She studied him. 'Instinct tells me we've reached the real reason for your visit. You didn't seek my sympathy when you came here, you sought an answer.'

'Is it correct that Señor Robson suffered badly from hay fever?'

'At times, yes, he did. I can remember soon after I met him suggesting he saw a specialist. I was informed, quite sharply, that he'd consulted more specialists than a spider has legs and none of them had done him much good. But that he'd been recommended a new kind of antihistamine pill and he was going to try that to see if it was any better than all the others . . . As luck would have it, it was.'

'Did he take a large number of these pills?'

'I can't answer that. Typically male, he seemed to think that swallowing a pill was a sign of weakness and only did so when no one was looking. Why on earth are you so interested in his hay fever?'

'I'm certain that someone exchanged pure heroin for the antihistamine in one of his pills.'

'My God! Who? Why?'

He shirked answering her, uncertain how distressed she would be to know the truth. 'You saw him on the Friday before he was taken ill, didn't you?'

'In the morning.'

'Would you think he was taking pills then?'

'I doubt it because he hadn't been sneezing or snuffling for several days.' She paused, then said: 'Only the fact is, isn't it, that that doesn't signify anything? Perhaps he didn't appear to be suffering because he'd been taking the pills out of sight . . . I just don't know.' She looked directly at him. 'Are you saying I might have been there when . . .' She trailed off into silence.

'If he'd swallowed the fatal pill on Friday morning, it would have affected him long before Saturday. He must have taken it on the Saturday, probably soon after waking up.'

'Thank goodness for that. If I thought . . . It's silly, I suppose, to worry whether I was there at the time. I didn't know, so the fact I did nothing couldn't give me the slightest reason for feeling guilty. Only when that sort of thing happens . . .' She shivered. 'Can we talk about something else?'

'In just one moment. But first I must ask you one thing more. Did he ever mention Sir John and Lady Varley?'

'The man who's minister of something?'

'That's right.'

She relaxed, managed a smile. 'You've jolted a memory. Yes, he did.'

He waited, but she remained silent. 'In what connection?'

She started. 'I'm sorry, I'd drifted off into the past . . . It was when he was here one afternoon. I had to mend a frock before we went out and while he waited, he leafed through some magazines. Very suddenly, he shouted: "That bitch!" Made me jab the needle into my finger.'

'He was referring to Lady Varley?'

'That's right. And it was the mildest of the terms he used. Which intrigued me no end because normally he didn't swear in front of women. He could be very old-fashioned.'

'Did you ask him what it was all about?'

'Of course. And when he didn't answer, I went over to see whose picture he was looking at.'

'Lady Varley?'

'A full length photo of her and her husband at some charity ball. I must admit, I thought his descriptions were probably very apt. She was wearing a gown that needed someone far more alive inside it and looking as if it was very hard work, mixing with the proles. In contrast, her husband looked as if he really did like helping people who needed help.'

'Did the señor tell you why her photo so annoyed him?'

'Not a word on the subject. In fact, when I teased him about it he began to get quite ratty and I had to stop. And that's all I know. So now you can tell me how she comes into things?'

'I believe she is the last piece in the puzzle.'

'You know that because Hugh called Lady Varley a bitch?'

'Yes.'

'And you know who killed Hugh and why?'

'Yes.'

'Then tell me.'

He shook his head. 'I have to check facts before I say anything to anyone.'

'Am I just anyone?'

'In this context—and this alone—I am afraid that is so.'

'Not even a hint?'

'Not even the hint of a hint.'

'What a stubborn man you can be.'

'A peasant has to learn to be stubborn if he is to survive.'

'A very poor smoke screen! "Peasant" often means stupid as well as stubborn and you call yourself a peasant when you need time to think and don't want others to realize how far from stupid you really are. Isn't that the truth?'

'I . . . I don't know.'

'I've embarrassed you! Good. I hope you're squirming . . . Your glass is empty and being the perfect hostess, I don't mind embarrassing you, but I won't have you thirsty.' She crossed to stand by the side of his chair. 'Give me your glass.'

He thought how simple it would be to reach out to her silken flesh . . . He handed her the glass. As she crossed to the sideboard, he said: 'Do you still have the magazine that the señor was looking at?'

'You said just one more question and since then you've asked a dozen.'

'It's just . . .'

'Just that your one is very elastic? . . . Yes, the magazines are still around because my lease said I had to leave this place exactly as I found it, they were here when I arrived, and someone told me that the landlord is the kind of man who takes that sort of a clause to the extreme.'

'If you ever have any problem with him, tell me. Then you will have no problem, of that I assure you.'

'What it is to have friends in high places!' She carried his glass back and handed it to him.

'Would it be easy to find the magazine with the photograph?'

'One moment the verray parfit gentil knight, the next the hawk-eyed sleuth. You're a chameleon who changes character, not colour. Which makes you bewildering to a one-character person like myself.' She crossed to a small bookcase which contained a pile of magazines as well as a number of paperbacks. She carried the magazines on to the dining-room table, began to look through them. 'I'm certain it was in one of the colour supplements. And on the cover was a caricature of the Prime Minister. Or was it a photograph? With him, it's difficult to distinguish one from t'other . . . Here's the Prime Minister. So now to discover.' She turned the pages. 'Supermodels, superstuds, and blood red Ferraris. How to grow oranges in Yorkshire—doesn't that strike you as rather a perverse ambition? Ten ways to make the tax man happy. A worse than perverse desire . . . Here we are. The photo that proves I am a memory genius.' She looked down at the opened page. 'A bitch without question, but a classical bitch! A walking encyclopædia of social do's and don't's: a woman on whom the sun never shines.' She carried the magazine over to him.

Sir John and Lady Varley were in evening dress, attending a charity ball. The previous time Alvarez had seen him, he'd been wearing nothing and performing specialized acrobatics.

'You're suddenly looking very sad, Enrique.'

It had to be a saddening experience to see an ideal shattered.

'I must leave,' he said.

'Why?' she asked.

On the face of things, it could not have been a simpler question. Yet for him it was filled with ambiguity. Was she suggesting, whilst not being specific, that he stay longer; if so, was this because she was feeling lonely and sought to keep his company a little longer or because she did not want him to leave before the morning? . . . He realized he lacked the courage to determine what was the correct answer. Could there be a more risible figure than the man who fooled himself into believing that a woman younger than he found maturity more attractive than youth? 'I have a lot of work to do.'

'At this time of the evening? You're making that up. Something about the photo has upset you so much you have to get away to be on your own to think about it.'

'Perhaps.'

'Then I wish I'd pretended I couldn't find it.'

He stood. 'Good night.'

'I'm afraid it's also au revoir.'

'What?'

'My money's almost run out and so I've had to book a flight whilst I could still just afford it. I'm flying home tomorrow morning to stay with my second cousin in Axted until I find a job and a flat.'

'Why not look for a job here . . .'

'And risk spoiling the memories?' She shook her head. 'They've been sad and they've been glad but recently, all glad. If I stayed on and failed to find a job because the labour market's so difficult and I'm a foreigner, things would start to go sour. I'd become just another lotus eater who'd dined too well. Then the later memories as well as some of the earlier ones would begin to hurt. I don't want that to happen. But don't think I'm going to disappear, just like that. I said, au revoir, not goodbye. The moment I'm settled, I'll be in touch. That is . . .' She hesitated. 'That is, if you want me to be?'

'Life will be empty until you speak.'

'That's the sweetest thing anyone's said to me. And so very un-peasant-like!'

He left the house, sad that she was leaving; happy that she so obviously wanted to see him again as soon as possible.

CHAPTER 21

When Alvarez walked into the dining-room, he could judge from Dolores's expression what she was going to say.

'I suppose you've been down in the port?'

'That's right.'

Jaime looked at him, surprised by the robust tone in which he'd answered.

'With . . .' Dolores would not say the name.

'With Honor.'

Her expression tightened. Jaime's puzzlement grew as he wondered why Alvarez was being such a fool as not to do what he could to escape the worst of her disapproval. Too much brandy, no doubt.

Alvarez said: 'I have to make a phone call to England.'

'To England?' The thought of what that must cost was sufficiently alarming to divert her thoughts.

'They're an hour behind us, aren't they, so it shouldn't be too late to ring?'

Neither of them answered because neither knew.

He returned to the front room. He dialled international directory inquiries, gave Mrs Robson's name and address, and asked for the telephone number.

After several rings, a woman said: 'Eckinstone three-one-seven-four-five.'

'Señora Robson?'

'Speaking.'

'My name is Inspector Alvarez and I am ringing from Llueso, in Mallorca.'

'Presumably in connection with the death of my husband?'

Her tone had been brisk. He envisaged a woman who met life's pitfalls more firmly than most. 'I'm sorry to trouble you, Señora, but I need to know if you can answer a question.'

'When you pose it, I will tell you.'

'Did Señor Robson ever meet Sir John and Lady Varley?'

'What an extraordinary thing to ask!'

'It may seem so, but I assure you that the answer may be of the greatest possible importance.'

'The Varleys are acquaintances and occasionally we meet in the homes of mutual friends. On one occasion, my husband was with me.'

'Did anything happen at this meeting which greatly upset him?'

'Good God! How on earth have you come to hear about that evening?'

'About which evening, Señora?'

'Then you're not omniscient! . . . My late husband was, as you presumably have gathered since I mentioned the fact to the detective who came here some time ago, conscious of a social lacuna. A strange concern for a man who had attained so much and in a time when social conventions have become more and more hazy. Although I have wondered more than once, I've never come to any real conclusion as to why he suffered this—marriage did not lead to an understanding of him. As a consequence, there were times when he became very ill at ease, almost to the point of panic, and he tried to cover up that fact by aggressive self-aggrandizement.

'Sir John is, to use a very old-fashioned expression, an English gentleman. His wife, while undoubtedly an English lady in the strictest sense, is very much more conscious of her position in life and has only scorn for those she considers parvenus. So when my husband was seated next to her at dinner, it was almost inevitable that sooner or later he would earn her contempt. It turned out to be sooner. During one of the lulls in conversation which are said to signal angels passing overhead, but in this case were more likely to have been mischievous devils, everyone present, including the servants, heard her express her opinion of him in the most cutting, most insultingly polite terms imaginable. The effect was quite extraordinary. He insisted on leaving as soon as the meal was over and when we were back home, he drank himself insensible—the first and only time I suffered such an experience. For weeks afterwards, he did his best to avoid social affairs on one or other excuse, but it was obvious that he imagined everyone was laughing at him. He lacked the rounded wit to realize that the sympathies of most people would lie with him because Lady Varley's standing as a prime bitch had long been unchallenged ... The whole incident showed so clearly how something of no real consequence whatsoever can occasionally cause greater distress than something of very considerable consequence. Is this what you wished to know, Inspector?'

'Yes, Señora.'

'How can something so inconsequential possibly have had anything to do with his death?'

'In a sense, it had everything. But at the moment, I fear I cannot explain why.'

He thanked her for her frank help and rang off. Absentmindedly, he lit a cigarette. To be a detective was to learn that in most humans the sublime and the ridiculous were bedfellows. Because Robson believed he'd been publicly humiliated by Lady Varley, he had set out to gain a vicious revenge.

He might have met Bridget and through her indiscretion have learned that Sir John was another of her clients; perhaps more likely, he might have garnered rumours about

Sir John's extra-marital pleasures and used her to entrap him. Whatever, Sir John had been drawn into the web and the video had been made. Eventually, Robson's aim would have been to cause Lady Varley even greater humiliation than he believed he had suffered at her hands, but he'd understood the secret of revenge—the longer, the sweeter. So initially, he'd conducted what had appeared to be a traditional form of blackmail. Only when that finally palled, had he intended to have the video circulated, thereby destroying her standing in society with mockery. But murder had cut short his revenge . . .

Alvarez returned to the dining-room, sat, and reached across for the bottle of 103. Yet could even brandy comfort someone who had had it confirmed yet again that while man's capacity for good was limited, for evil it was unlimited?

Now that the nights were warm, he wore only pyjama trousers in bed. With the sheet drawn up no higher than his waist, he stared up at the ceiling. From the beginning, he had instinctively known that the key to this case was motive, but from the moment blackmail seemed to be that motive, he had been troubled by the paradox of a rich man engaging in it. Now there was no longer a paradox because Robson had been blackmailing to gain revenge, not money . . . From the beginning, he had logically looked at the murders of Bridget and Robson in chronological order. Now he knew that the first had been last and the last had been first. Logically, since Mills had died before Bridget and Bridget before Robson, that was the order in which they'd been murdered. But if one were prepared to view the murders illogically, this wasn't necessarily so.

Bridget and Mills had fallen in love—surely on the face of things as illogical as anything in the case? Even so, they'd remained sufficiently practical to accept that love alone did not feed, warm, and house the body as well as the soul. So he'd decided—almost certainly against her advice—to visit Robson to demand more money, with the threat of exposure if this were refused. As he'd been sent by his firm to try to recover the tape, erroneously thought to be in her possession, he was in a position to do so without danger to himself or to Bridget. Robson, however, had recognized that blackmail for money never came to an end—whatever was promised—until there was no more money left and then the blackmailer might, resentful that his income was lost, expose his victim. So for Robson there could be only one avenue of escape—the deaths of Mills and Bridget.

He had shot Mills and dumped the body in the mountains where it was reasonable to suppose—when one did not know the Mallorquin hunter—it would not be found for some time, perhaps even until positive identification was impossible. That done, he'd flown to Barcelona, hired a white Escort and driven to La Malon Haute. There, he'd spoken to Bridget and, exerting his very considerable charm, had explained that he'd talked things over with Mills and they'd decided he should come to France to discuss with her how best to manage the blackmail in the future so that all three of them benefitted.

She was streetwise, which Mills had not been. She had also had reason to recognize that under Robson's friendly, warm, jovial character there lurked hard ruthlessness, which was why she'd been so against Mills's trip. And so when Mills had failed to telephone to say how things were progressing, she'd become worried; when Robson had turned up on his own, she'd become terrified. As soon as he'd left the house, she'd telephoned the hotel in which Mills had been staying and had learned that he had vanished, leaving his bill unpaid. That had been enough to convince her that he had been murdered.

She was a woman who had experienced the darkest side

of life, but had then unexpectedly been lifted to its heights when she found love. Robson had murdered her lover; her bitter, broken-hearted passion demanded that he, in turn, be murdered.

Despite her desperate desire for revenge, she had recognized the need to cover her guilt in Robson's murder. She could be certain he would be back in order to judge whether she was suspicious of him and so becoming a threat and that would provide her with her opportunity. But how to murder him so that she did not immediately become the main suspect? During her time, had she learned of a murderer who had successfully devised a method of killing his victim without danger to himself; had her passionate hatred inspired her to devise her own 'perfect' murder? No one would ever now know.

She had chosen heroin as her poison. Because drugs and prostitution so often went together, she had had some in her possession or known where to buy locally. She might have purified what she had, but the forensic laboratory had termed the operation a laborious one and she had had little time. Far more likely—remembering that she had left the house that afternoon in a rush and had driven to Auchoise—that she had known who in that town could supply pure heroin.

Her judgement of Robson had been both correct and fatally incorrect. He had returned, ostensibly to continue the discussion, in fact to murder her. But wanting to make her murder look like an accident, he had moved slowly, allowing her mistakenly to believe she was staying one jump ahead of him, as she used all her wiles to arouse his passions and then assuage them, thereby providing her with the opportunity to exchange the contents of one of the antihistamine capsules which she knew he always carried about with him . . .

He had died twelve days after he had murdered her. But she had murdered him.

Alvarez turned his head to stare at the cupboard inside which was the strong-box. The video had been responsible for three deaths. He would show that it had not yet exhausted its capacity to hurt. Lady Varley would discover that she also was going to have to pay a high price for having been connected, however indirectly, with the case.

CHAPTER 22

'Enrique,' Dolores said, 'only a fool races after a second rainbow.'

He looked up from the mug of hot chocolate. 'What are you on about?'

'For days you've done nothing but sit about the house, all miserable.'

'D'you expect me to look like I've won the primitive lottery? Maybe you've forgotten that I've been suspended from work and am booked for a dishonourable discharge?'

'Does that stop you going out and about? You could help Inés with the work on her finca.'

'I could, but I'm not going to.'

'Why not?'

'Her second son still lives with her.'

'Maybe he is a difficult lad sometimes . . .'

'Bloody impossible, all the time.'

'All he needs is a firm hand.'

'She snores like a donkey.'

'How do you know that?' she asked, suddenly hopeful.

'Miguel told me, not long before he died.'

'Men are such pigs!' she said furiously. She picked up her purse and shopping bag and left.

He finished the coca. Inés's finca was large and productive. If only she did not snore and have a younger son who epitomized the perils of parenthood . . . His mind switched tracks. Sir John Varley, held in such high esteem by all, was about to be exposed as a notable hypocrite even by English standards. Revenge was going to be very sweet indeed. It was going to teach that bitch of a wife that all her rank and fortune did not entitle her to bear false witness and wreck the career of a Mallorquin inspector to whom she'd spoken as if he were a one-eyed beggar from the caves of Seville . . .

The phone interrupted his thoughts.

'I have a message from the Superior Chief,' said the secretary, even more plum-voiced than usual. 'The disciplinary hearing will take place at ten o'clock next Thursday, the seventeenth, at the headquarters of Armada y Trafico. Do you understand?'

'Yes, Señorita.'

He returned to the dining-room where he collected a bottle of brandy, then continued through to the kitchen. He sat, added brandy to the chocolate until the mug was once more full. On Thursday, his career would come to an end even though every action he had taken had been motivated by the best of intentions. The Director-General sought perverse recompense for the rollocking he had received from the Minister of the Interior, Salas for the rollocking he'd received from the Director-General. It had ever been thus. It had ever been unfair.

He finished the chocolate, poured out a little more brandy. And as he swallowed the last mouthful, he suddenly realized something. He intended to be just as unfair to another as he was claiming others had been unfair to him. Lady Varley was the cause of his misfortunes, not her husband. Further, it would not be only Sir John who would unjustly suffer. So would all those who saw in him an ideal to be admired. Better never to have an ideal than see one destroyed. Sometimes a myth could be more important than the reality.

Once he'd managed to clear his mind of false passions, he could clearly see what he had to do. He could, of course, ill afford to do it and he would receive curses, not thanks— no man liked to be placed under an obligation—but he must travel to England and hand the tape to Sir John Varley.

As he climbed out of the hired car, a policeman in uniform walked up. ''Morning.'

Because of the tone, it had been a question as well as a greeting. 'I'm Inspector Alvarez, from Mallorca. I should like to speak to Sir John Varley.'

'Sorry to have to ask, sir, but do you have identification?'

It was not the first time that his rank of 'inspector' had earned him a 'sir' in England. He showed his warrant card.

The front door was opened by the butler who looked at him with the same distaste as before and said that Sir John was not at home.

'But I spoke to someone in London who told me he would be here today and tomorrow.'

'Not at home,' explained the butler, contemptuous of the ignorance of foreigners, 'means he's not at home to those he does not wish to be at home to.'

It was a weird language. 'Would you please tell him I've come from Mallorca especially to see him in connection with inquiries made by Ponsonby and Braithwaite.'

The butler hesitated, then shut the door in his face.

The PC walked up. 'Having trouble?'

'The butler said Sir John is not at home but that seems to mean he is, only the butler doesn't think he'll wish to talk to me.'

'The butler, sir, wants a kick up the you-know-what.'

The door was opened once more. 'Sir John will give you five minutes, no more,' said the butler sulkily.

Alvarez followed him across the hall, down a corridor, and into the library, a large room in which three walls were lined with books. Sir John Varley stood to the side of a handsome desk, in front of a single window.

In his own domain—as opposed to appearing on tape— he was the quintessential Englishman, Alvarez thought. Tall and slim, wearing a suit that fitted like an outer skin; a maturely handsome, strongly featured face that expressed both the self-confidence of a man totally at peace with himself and the humour which prevented that self-confidence becoming self-satisfaction. The kind of person whose sense of honour had, before the days of mass travel, been so respected that when Spaniards had wanted to show the greatest faith towards each other, they had made their promises on 'the word of an Englishman'. 'Good morning, Sir John.'

Varley waited until the butler had left, then said, his tone clipped: 'What do you want?'

'I am here to give you something, Señor.'

He looked at the padded envelope in Alvarez's hand. 'What, precisely?'

Alvarez brought the videotape out of the envelope and stepped forward to put it on the desk.

Varley stared at it for several seconds, then walked over to the window and looked out. 'I am a very busy man and do not have the time to bargain.' His voice had been hard and steady, but when he next spoke, it held a slight quiver. 'How much do you want now?'

'I don't quite understand.'

'Come on, man, there's no need to beat about the bush. How much am I going to have to pay to prevent the publication of the original of that videotape?'

'Sir John, I have come to give, not to sell.'

Varley, his face drawn, swung round. 'You are not here to demand more money than before?'

'No.'

'You really . . .' He became silent as his expression changed. Then he said, in tones of bleak despair: 'Since the age of miracles is long past, I am being naïve. That is either a blank or a copy. The original remains safely hidden. And although you are not demanding more money, you will not refuse an offer of such. Is that not a correct summation of the position?'

'This is the original tape and as far as I know, no copies of it exist.'

'How have you, a policeman, come into possession of it?'

'I found it in the possession of Señor Robson, the man who was blackmailing you and who was murdered. My Superior Chief left it in my hands and so I decided that it should be handed to you.'

He crossed to the desk, went to pick up the tape, but at the last moment withdrew his hand. 'Why did you make that decision?'

'I have heard you referred to as the only truly honest politician in the country, by someone who clearly had no reason to like your politics. I believe you must be a person whom many respect. In a time when so few are respected, to disillusion many would be very sad.'

'I may be honest financially and politically, but this tape proves that I am morally dishonest.'

'That is for you alone to consider.'

He ran his hand over his silver-grey hair. 'I wonder if you can understand . . . I feel the urge to try to explain and so excuse my actions, but since to most they are probably inexplicable and certainly inexcusable, that would be a waste of time. In any case, I judge you to be one of the few for whom such an explanation would be meaningless because you are too humane to believe in conventional boundaries. However, what I can do is apologize, most sincerely, for having assumed that you had come here to increase the blackmail to which I have been subject.' He opened the top right-hand drawer of the desk and dropped the tape into it. As he closed the drawer and locked it, he said: 'I should be grateful if you'd have lunch with me later this week when I am in London?'

'I am afraid . . .'

'I hasten to add that the invitation is not an attempt to repay even a tithe of what you have given me. I am asking you to show even more generosity by allowing me to ease some of the sense of guilt I feel for having so crassly misjudged you.'

'Sir John, nothing would give me greater pleasure than to accept, but I have to fly back to Mallorca tomorrow.'

'Flights can easily be transferred.'

'I must be in Palma on Thursday morning to appear before a disciplinary hearing.'

'Which is being held as a consequence of what?'

'I fear that my previous visit to this house did not proceed altogether smoothly and a complaint about it was made to the Spanish ambassador; by the time the complaint reached my Superior Chief, it appeared that I had been exceedingly rude to your wife. In addition, I forgot to ask my Superior Chief for his permission and authority to fly from France to England or to seek the necessary permission to conduct an investigation in this country.'

'It would appear that you work in somewhat unconventional ways.'

'My Superior Chief would very much agree with you, Sir John.'

There was a short silence. Then Varley said: 'I am very sorry, but I really am a busy man and so must say goodbye.' He came round the desk and shook hands. 'Perhaps the thanks you will most appreciate is for me to say that you

have restored my faith not only in human nature, but also,
in part, in myself.'

Alvarez sat on the right-hand bed in the hotel bedroom
and stared at the telephone. All Honor had said was that
she'd be staying with second cousins in Axted. Only if they
were on her paternal side would they have the same surname . . . She had been back in England less than a week.
So however much she might eventually want to see him
again, this might well be too soon . . .

It was asking too much of him not to try to talk to her
and arrange a meeting. He phoned directory inquiries and
explained that he was trying to trace a family called Seymour who lived in Axted, but he did not know their address.
In the circumstances, it was probably too much to ask, but
as he had to return home, to Mallorca, the next day, was
there any chance . . . The woman he spoke to was very
helpful; she told him there were eleven Seymours listed in
Axted and gave him the numbers.

He phoned. One person thought he was selling and cut
short the call, another initially mistook him for a friend
from Chile. But the seventh person he spoke to, a woman
with a low pitched voice, said: 'Yes, my husband has a
distant cousin whose name is Honor.'

'And she has been living in Mallorca for the past few
months?'

'As far as I know.'

'May I speak with her, please?'

'She's not here.'

'Then she has already found a flat? Perhaps you will be
kind enough to give me the telephone number of that?'

'I'm not certain that after all we are talking about the
same person. I haven't seen Honor in several months; not
since some time before she went abroad, in fact. We're

friendly enough, but regretfully don't keep in as close contact as perhaps we should.'

'Señora, one more question will make certain whether
she is the same person. Did the mother of your husband's
second cousin recently die after a long illness?'

'Yes, she did. Very sad, even if it was a merciful release
for Honor as well for her.'

'She must be the same Honor! Yet she told me only a
few days ago that she would be staying with you until she
found a flat and a job.'

'As I said a moment ago, I haven't seen or heard from
her in quite a time.'

'Are you sure?'

'Of course I am. I imagine you must have misunderstood
her.'

'I surely did not, Señora.'

A note of exasperation crept into her voice and her words
made it clear she was someone who was often very direct.
'Then perhaps you should consider the possibility that she
said what she did because she'd decided she did not want
to continue the friendship.'

'If that were the case, why should she have mentioned
your correct name and where you live?'

'I really have no idea.'

He stared at the wall, covered in a dark wallpaper. Why
on earth should Honor have lied about her future intentions, yet in such a way that he would uncover that lie if
he tried to get in touch with her? Only one answer came
to mind and to accept that . . . His voice was strained when
he asked: 'From what illness did Honor's mother die?'

'I fail to see how that can be of any concern to you.'

'Señora, as well as being a friend of Honor's, I am a
detective.'

After a while, she said: 'Are you implying that the circumstances of Mary's death are of concern to you in your professional capacity?'

'I first met Honor because she was the friend of a man whose murder I was investigating.'

'My God!'

'And it is possible that the answer to my question to you will prove to be of considerable consequence to my investigation. What illness did Señora Seymour die from?'

'It wasn't exactly an illness in the accepted sense. The man she married a long time ago was a rotter and treated her abominably. Mary wasn't, to tell the truth, as strong a character as she needed to be and after he'd deserted her, she started drinking heavily and taking drugs. Things went from bad to worse, but Honor looked after her right up to the end. This probably sounds melodramatic, but there's something of the saint in Honor.'

A saint had once been defined as someone who lacked the courage to be a sinner. 'I have just one more question, Señora. What work did Honor do before her mother died and she came to Mallorca?'

'She was a laboratory assistant in a firm whose headquarters are in London. They must have rated her work highly because she told me that they tried hard to persuade her to accept promotion. I couldn't understand why she didn't take it.'

He thanked her for her help and rang off. He lit a cigarette and wished he could stretch out his hand and pick up a bottle of Soberano and drink it empty in an attempt to anaesthetize his mind, even if only temporarily. But he couldn't, so he remembered that Honor never touched alcohol—often a sign of alcohol-related problems in the past; that although other women had found Robson's combination of charm and wealth irresistible, she had resisted it, but so cleverly that he hadn't realized the extent to which she had and he had determined to divorce his wife in order

to be free to marry her; that there'd been the time when
he, Alvarez, had told her that Robson had stolen all his
first wife's money and left her penniless and with a child
to bring up and moments later Honor had correctly identified the child as a daughter . . . She was that daughter.

He had said to Salas that he was instinctively certain
that motive was the prime clue to solving the death of
Robson. Discover the motive and one would have identified
the murderer. Unfortunately, he'd forgotten something
more that he'd said—the true motive might well be more
obscure than the facts of the case. He should have realized
that when he'd unearthed a straightforward motive—
blackmail—he should have dug deeper to discover if there
was another, hidden one.

When a person committed a crime, his or her best chance
of escaping conviction was to provide an apparently
unshakeable alibi. If the victim died at midnight, 'prove'
one was elsewhere at that time. But what if one did not
know when the murder would actually take place? Then
clearly an alibi of time must be useless. But an alibi of
character could provide insurance because if one had
known only good of a person, why on earth should one
have murdered him? Everyone but Honor had noticed at
least some of the fault lines in Robson's character; she had
apparently noticed none, even though she had proved herself to be a sharp, perceptive judge of character . . .

He wished he could not now remember what every detective was taught never to forget. Fit the theory to the facts,
not the facts to the theory. Then he could still believe that
Bridget had been sufficiently sharp and intelligent to be
alive to her danger and to have decided on a pre-emptive
strike; that she'd been able to find at short notice a dealer
in Auchoise who'd sell her pure heroin. But now he knew
that she had been far from a sharp and intelligent murderer—which could and should have been deduced from

the facts that she had stayed in La Malon Haute when clearly life there had bored her and that the post-mortem had made no reference to drug taking, which it almost certainly would have done had she been an addict. If not an addict, how would she have known where to find a dealer who would sell her pure heroin? The truth was, Robson had used his charm to such effect that she'd been blinded to her danger and her trip to Auchoise had not been to buy heroin, but probably some special delicacy which she knew he liked and was not available locally. When her eyes were opened it was only to have them closed for ever.

Honor had given him the name of her cousin. Why? Merely to add casual veracity to the reason she gave for leaving the island so suddenly? Or because she had judged that sooner or later he must try to contact her and when he spoke to Mrs Seymour he would finally realize the truth; and then he would not expose her as the murderer of Robson because not only must all his sympathies lie with her, she had woven her spell so expertly that he could never condemn her to trial and imprisonment?

He would have given anything to erase from time the phone call to Mrs Seymour. But only the gods could destroy the past.

CHAPTER 23

Alvarez waited in the small, dusty, rather smelly room that lacked a window, and dismally wondered if his judges had yet decided on his punishment? Would they be satisfied with dismissing him from the force with ignominy—and without a pension—or would Salas have persuaded them that where so heinous a crime was concerned, there should be no mercy?

The door opened and a man, whom he'd never seen before, entered. 'Inspector Alvarez?'

'Señor.' He squared his shoulders and tightened his stomach muscles. A Spaniard might not know how to live but, by God, he knew how to die!

'My name is Comisario Giminez. I have flown in from Madrid.' He came forward and shook hands.

The politeness bewildered him.

'It is my pleasant task to inform you that the Director-General has received from England a personal letter from Don Sir Varley, a minister of the British Crown. In this letter, Don Sir Varley refers to the complaint that was made to our ambassador in London. He states that he has subsequently learned that this complaint was mistaken in every respect and that there is absolutely no cause for you to be censured; to the contrary, there is good reason for you to be praised for the style in which you conducted the original interview. He adds that you also showed tact and discretion far above that which might normally be expected in the subsequent meeting with him and he was particularly struck by the manner in which you brought unlimited credit to the Cuerpo General de Policia. In view of this he asks as a personal favour . . .' Giminez rolled the words 'personal favour' around on his tongue, 'that should you, in the best interests of all concerned, perhaps have not adhered strictly to the rules and regulations, that you be excused any blame or penalty. The Director-General has informed Don Sir Varley that he is happy to accede to this request.'

Alvarez's initial sense of disbelief was so great that he silently echoed the sixteenth-century Marqués de Ribol's comment on first seeing a rhinoceros—a comment so obscene that for centuries there had been acrimonious dispute as to whether so noble a man could actually have used such debased language.

'We will now go into the next room where, on the orders of the Director-General, a personal commendation will be read aloud by your Superior Chief.'

As Alvarez walked through to the next room, his bewilderment was so great that he felt as if in the middle of a dream. No disciplinary hearing, no finding of guilty, no dismissal with ignominy, no loss of pension? . . . And then he saw Salas's expression. Not even a nightmare could have pictured such suppressed fury. This was for real. For the first time in days, he felt he might smile again.